I0822303

Faeted to the Clawed Throne One

ADALYND GRAYVES

Book Cover by Lewellen Designs

Illustrations by Wanderlust Ink

1st edition 2023

GIVEN TO THE WOLF KING

Two kingdoms share a single curse. Can a princess and a king come together to save their people?

Facing trial for a crime she didn't commit. Aoife knows she must put her duty as the fae princess before her own freedom and leave Erainn- the home she so fiercely loves and wants to protect.

A darkness is infecting both fae and human kingdoms alike. Only by accepting her father's command to live with the Wolf King in Nairn can she discover what or who is causing it. Feeling suffocated and trapped on castle grounds, she looks for a way to escape, but finds herself developing feelings for the king and ultimately decides to stay.

Cullen knows the alliance between Erainn and Nairn protects his people, but many say the fae cannot be trusted. With hatred growing between the two kingdoms, he does what he thinks is right and takes Aoife as his ward. While there is no hard evidence to prove her crime, he sees a darkness in her, but this doesn't stop his budding feelings for the fae princess.

Faced with plotting enemies, and the curse spreading. Can Cullen and Aoife set aside their differences to bring their kingdoms together in peace? Will they give in to their true feelings?

Content Awareness. This is a slow burn, enemies to lovers' romantic fantasy that addresses darker themes with a guaranteed HFN. *This story takes place in a fantasy world of the author's making.*

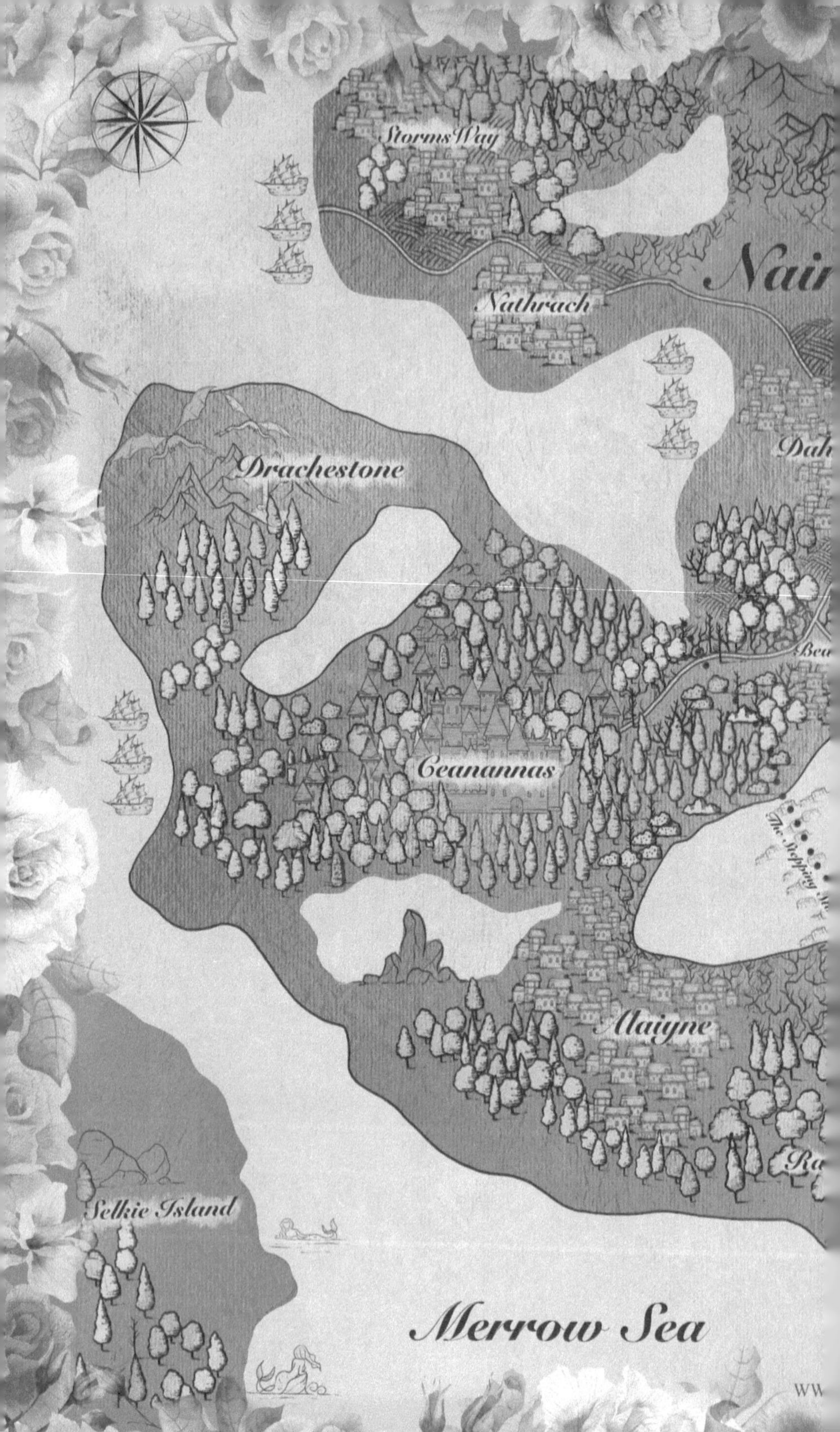

Storms Way
Nathrach
Nai
Dah
Drachestone
Ceanannas
The Stepping
Alaiyne
Selkie Island
Merrow Sea

Drothailte
(Badlands)
Gateway to
Realm of Faery
The Curse
Kirkwall
The gorge
Daithe
Stonnhaven
Stonnhaven Castle
Mora
Thorn
Bregdi Seabane
World of
Eavelaen

ONE

AOIFE

The Unaligned Princess

"Aoife, Aoife... Aoife! Where is that girl?" Orla's shrill voice echoed through the palace gardens as Aoife made her way to her favorite hiding spot.

She caught sight of periwinkle fabric out of the corner of her eye and quickly hid behind the Elder Tree's gnarled trunk, pressing her body against its worn bark. She exhaled, the tension in her shoulders relaxing as she sank into the tree's embrace. All she wanted was a few stolen moments of stillness before returning to the chaos of court life.

Eyes closed, Aoife splayed her palms against the

trunk, feeling the tree's ancient energy thrumming beneath her fingertips. But her concentration shattered at the crunch of footsteps drawing near, accompanied by Orla's gravelly tone.

"Aoife, by all the fae, if you don't come here at once, I'll send the guards... and your twin brother after you!"

Aoife peeked around the tree to see Orla storming down the garden path as the glitz of diamonds danced off the surrounding shrubs. Her ruse was up. She slipped out from her refuge to see her godsmother storming toward her in a blue hued rage.

"Young lady! You're not a sapling anymore! Your duty is to attend to the needs of our domain. The court is waiting! Do you want the Elders to think you're irresponsible? You better be in that gown I sat out for you!"

Reluctantly, Aoife drug her hand away from the tree's touch. *Sorry my friend, I'll be back to visit you later.* Squaring her shoulders, she turned and faced Orla, who positioned herself in front of Aoife. The old woman's brows pinched, her violet eyes stark and hard, with lips drawn tight into a frown. The rigidity of Orla's expression stood out against her silvery strands of satiny curled locks that hugged her soft, wrinkled cheeks.

Aoife crossed her left arm over her chest, then her

right, and gave a small, respectful bow. "Godsmother, I was collecting my thoughts before the meeting. I am not late."

Orla's nostrils flared. "You have five minutes until the conclave begins, Princess. In my book, that's late."

Aoife took a slow, calming breath. "Godsmother, I still have nine minutes to spare. There is no need for such dramatics. The assembly is two minutes away."

Orla's frown deepened with her response and Aoife swore she saw lavender flames flick around the edges of her irises. She shivered beneath the intensity of her godsmother's piercing gaze. It was hard for her to understand how such a friendly face adorned such cold eyes. Her signature pink silk slippers also contrasted with her otherwise fierce presence. Despite her gentle features, it was always clear Orla meant business.

"Efi, you're being difficult," Orla chided.

"I'm trying to prepare myself after a long patrol, Godsmother," Aoife replied evenly. "You know these conclaves wear on me."

Orla clicked her tongue. "So formal today, I see." Some bite remained in her tone. She'd have to tread lightly.

Efi sighed, "Ma. You're well aware I have every intention of attending. I don't need you to reprimand or patronize me beforehand."

Orla's face softened. "Of course not dear. Come here. Let me have a look at you. Please tell me you let Yseult dress you today."

Aoife grimaced. "She did my hair. But I don't see why Father and you insist I need a lady's maid. I can dress myself perfectly fine."

Orla rolled her eyes skyward. "You're impossible. Take your station more seriously, please."

Aoife bit back a sharp retort, knowing that provoking Orla could make matters worse. "I didn't ask for this. No one asked if I wanted to be a princess. Yet I've accepted and adjusted the best I could."

"Well, to that, I say you better adjust more." Orla grumbled under her breath and stifled her next reaction with a heavy sigh.

Aoife silently stepped forward, head down, before she spun around so Orla could inspect the gown. The silky olive-green complimented her complexion.

While dresses had never been her first choice of attire, this one was stunning. The fabric hugged her waist perfectly, loosely cascading down to the ground.

A detailed embroidered design with sparkling green gems threaded in matched the color of the dress itself: a swirling pattern of delicate leaves and flowers spread across her chest and encircled the edges of each bell-sleeve. The hem of the dress was shaped into the point of petals or leaves. The perfect needlework then wrapped around her hips—traveling down to her thighs and ended right above her knees.

Despite her reservations in the beginning, Aoife loved the dress and wasted no time in showing her appreciation to Orla. "Thank you for choosing out this gown for me... truly my favorite so far."

Orla's face softened, and she looked somewhat appeased, though one eyebrow crooked up. "Don't think sweet words will work on me young lady." But her previous tone had lost its edge.

"Godsmother, I'm not trying to do anything. I am grateful you picked this out for me and I am honored to wear it. I'd love to see more dresses like this too. Please. I'll say it again. Thank you."

Orla gave her a once over, a small smile forming where there was a previous frown. With a curt nod, Orla shooed her away in the palace's direction. "Off with ya."

Efi straightened her back before walking away. These sessions were the worst part of her day. Especially when she had to listen to the same ramblings of the unaligned Elders' Conclave as they postulated on the Dark Fae invading.

She thought it was pointless to focus on something that had little chance of occurring. Her people had left the fae world over three hundred years ago and had established a kingdom of their own. The Light Fae had long given up forcing the inhabitants of Erainn back into the realms of Faery. So why would the Dark Fae be any different?

Yet, the fair folk's animosity toward her father was not lost on her. She understood the two courts were unlikely to forget and above all forgive. Her tutors made it clear he had played a significant role in their departure from Faery and the way Erainn, their kingdom, was shaped.

Their domain boasted a freedom the aligned fae would never experience. Every citizen was unaligned, meaning they had the freedom to choose how they lived their lives. The light & dark made their subjects choose a side, and in doing so, bound that fae to their strict rules and customs. She was grateful for her family's part in escaping, but she grew tired of hearing about the evil coming for them all someday.

Her father's words echoed in her mind: *The chances of the dark fae sneaking in to spy or inflicting damage are minuscule, but not impossible. We should be diligent in securing our borders always.*

There hadn't been a sighting of spies in eighty years. She wondered why they were making such a fuss when there were other matters to take care of.

It'd never happen, she told herself, before rounding a corner on the east side of the palace. She crawled to a halt when two large oak doors came into view.

Efi perked her ears up and grabbed the large golden leaf-shaped handle and pulled one door open. She slipped in quietly and took a seat before her father sauntered in with her eldest brother Cillian close behind.

The meeting began as soon as he sat down. The scouts detailed their report of border safety and trade with the humans. Despite the brief exchanges of her colleagues, Aoife lost herself in a daydream. She pictured herself free from royal duties. The sweet breeze of the ocean tickled her face. The seals surrounded her, and their sweet, melodic chatter filled her ears. With a mention of her name, she jolted and remembered the meeting.

"Aoife, how are the woodland areas getting along?" Her father's booming voice echoed against the small, confined space they all sat in.

Soon, all eyes were on her. She glanced around with stiff shoulders and cleared her throat. "My patrol and I have attended to the western territory, father. All was well and in order. No concerns need to be further addressed. Tomorrow, we'll travel east to ensure the flora and fauna on our side are safe," she spoke courteously.

Cillian scoffed and muttered under his breath. She didn't have to understand his words to discern his complaints about her lack of attention. Efi glared in his direction, her face hot with rage.

"Does my brother have a concern he needs to voice? *Is* there something I did not include in my report?" Efi tilted her gaze up and let her eyes connect to his. *Come on Cillian, I dare you.*

"Aye, my sister. What was said prior to your report?"

"What does it have to do with my patrol?" Aoife bit her lip. He was trying to make a fool out of her in front of everyone. *For what purpose? He's been my best friend for years.* Her father stood up with his hand out, motioning for him to stop.

"That is enough. Aoife's done well. Her love and care of our lands and the bordering sea are unmatched. Her attention to these matters has ensured the well-being of the environment beyond what the Conclave has imagined. Erainn has never been so prosperous before. We have Aoife to thank for that."

"Here, here! King Torin is right," Several of the Conclave agreed.

Efi cracked a small smile and kept her eyes on the ground. It was nice to hear they appreciated her work. She hated the confines of the palace and seldom spent time inside, save for the library. Hadn't

Cil understood how taxing this position had been for her?

"Father–I," Cillian began.

"Back to the matter at hand. We're done here. Aoife's was the last account for the day. At least for the time being. We must fulfill our assigned duties for the next month starting now. File all reports with *The Archivist* and proceed from there. We'll meet in two weeks' time to review progress."

The heavy oak doors of the council room creaked open as the Elders shuffled out in pairs and trios, their murmuring voices fading down the corridor. Aoife lingered behind, glancing over at her father and brother.

As soon as they were alone, Cillian rushed to her side and folded her into a gentle hug. She breathed in the familiar pine and vanilla scent of home that clung to him. He must have been in the old cabin before arriving at the palace.

It was always a peaceful place filled with their mother's warmth. Unlike the cold that drenched each crevice of the castle that Father had forced them to live in.

"Dearest sister," he said, voice muffled in her hair. "Now that we've both come of age, the duty of leading our people into the future falls to us. You must take your role in the Conclave seriously—they'll be looking to you now."

He pulled back, regret creasing his brow. "I apologize for needling you today. I know you're still adjusting to your new responsibilities. Can you forgive me?"

Aoife sighed, smoothing the wrinkles in her gown. "I wish you'd waited until after the session to voice your concerns. You know I'm struggling to find my footing."

Cillian's hands rested on her shoulders, his gaze intent on hers. "I know, and again, I'm sorry."

Their father stepped forward then, clearing his throat. "My children, you both stand on the cusp of adulthood. The next ten years will teach you much about leadership and sacrifice. Here in Erainn, we must adopt the ways of men, not the endless revelries of the fae. The peace between our peoples depends on it."

Aoife and her brother turned to their father and bowed their heads. "We understand, and we're ready," they affirmed in unison.

A grave look passed over the king's face. "I'm afraid a new trial has come sooner than expected. A matter I need kept quiet for now until we know more." His eyes flicked between them, brow raised, waiting for their assent.

They both nodded, Aoife adding, "Of course, Father."

"An emissary from the human kingdom has reported a vile black sludge seeping from the trees near our border. He followed its spread for miles as it poisoned field after field in its wake. I need my finest to investigate this threat. Cillian, take your scouts and accompany your sister."

Aoife furrowed her brow, confused. "But Father, if the damage is contained in Nairn, how are we affected?"

Her father sighed heavily. "We cannot discount anything that harms our human neighbors. Our fates are intertwined. If left unchecked, this poison could spread across the border through the ancient magics that bind our lands. We must act swiftly and without mercy, should the need arise."

"Then we'll leave at once!" Cillian and Efi spoke in unison.

"You two, so alike, yet so different. I can't think of anyone else more fit for the task. Now, this is where I bid you both farewell. Take your time, leave no stone nor branch unturned."

"Understood." Cil bowed.

"Yes, Father. We won't stop our search until we've dealt with it." Efi curtsied.

Torin's enormous arms wrapped around her in a

tight bear hug. "I love you, my little leaf. Please be careful and return safely to me." He squeezed her tighter. After all, she was his only daughter.

Cillian approached next. The embrace was harsher. A rough hug, pats on the back, and silence between the two.

Cil turned to her. "Meet you at the stables?"

"Yes."

They crossed their arms, heads bowed, then departed to get themselves ready for the journey. Aoife rushed to change into her dragon scaled armor, buckled her belt, and heard the satisfying click of her short sword as it slid into its hilt.

The armor was a gift from one of the dragon families. From the sheds of Ceddros, Lord of Fires himself. She never left the palace without the armor on. It was a rare gift meant to be appreciated with use and not squandered by display. There wasn't a set that matched its level of protection.

Aoife's boots clicked against the stone floors as she hurried through the palace kitchens, gathering supplies for the journey ahead. She inhaled the warm, yeasty aroma of freshly baked bread as she wrapped a loaf, still steaming from the oven, in a large scrap of cheesecloth. Added to it were a handful of rosy apples, a wedge of salty white cheese, and a sealed jar of honey butter, its golden contents gleaming temptingly through the glass.

She tucked the bundle securely into her leather pack before heading out. Her brother and his scouts met her at the entrance of the stables. Her horse, Caisearbhan, stood tethered to a post, outfitted, and waiting for her arrival. She greeted him fondly, running a hand along his muscular neck before mounting. With a click of her tongue, they set off toward the Eastern Forest, Caisearbhan's hooves clattering rhythmically on the cobblestones.

Her brother's scouts soon closed ranks around her, the clinking of their armor and weaponry announcing their approach. She knew some of the more seasoned rangers would scour ahead, scouting the path before the group, screening them from any hidden dangers. Aoife wasn't sure what they'd find when they arrived. The forest to the east shared a border with Nairn, the human kingdom—they had a three-hour ride's time remaining before they'd obtain any real answers.

They traveled down the ancient, weathered road dubbed the *Beaten Lane*—it wended its way through the heart of Erainn before crossing into the kingdom of Nairn.

The road led them straight from their palace city to the stronghold of the fearsome Wolf King. Aoife shuddered as she recalled the tales of his bestial ferocity, a great big man with a wolfish grin sitting upon his antlered and fur skinned throne.

The castle appeared as fierce as he was, or so she had been told. Long ago, his family had sculpted the castle into the very mountain with their bare hands. Magically molding it into the fortress as hard and unyielding as their king now.

They carved this castle from more than the stone of the mountain—tall shimmering obsidian monoliths towered above the city. And precious gemstones protruded out on all sides. Shimmering in the sunlight.

It was said that a rider could see the gleam miles before arriving and once there, they'd behold giant wolves etched into the slate gray stone walls with scenes of the hunt, pack life, and more covering every inch. Wolves themselves no longer roamed Erainn, but remained the sigil of the Nairn royalty, bringing to Aoife's mind savagery and blood.

Ever so often, she heard the wolves in Nairn howl when she camped near the border, and slivers of fear crawled up her spine. The contrasts between the two kingdoms were unmistakable. Wrinkling her nose in distaste, Aoife recalled watching the humans at work —their rough voices shouting and grunting as they felled trees with heavy axes. They seemed chaotic, destructive, tearing through the forest with no thought of replanting or nurturing the land they continued to ravage.

Her father often chided her disdain for them, but she struggled to understand his affection. In her eyes, humans were short-sighted in their relationship with nature. Perhaps it was no surprise one of their emissaries had brought word of a spreading poison... no doubt exacerbated by their carelessness.

After riding for two hours, Cillian called the company to a halt, directing them to water and rest their mounts. Aoife welcomed the respite, her legs aching from the relentless pace.

As the horses drank their fill from a trickling stream, she settled beneath the shade of a towering elm and retrieved the food bundle from her pack. Cillian plopped down beside her, eyes glinting eagerly as she unwrapped the treasure trove of delicacies filched from the palace kitchens.

"Efi to the rescue with delicious food!" Cil proclaimed, grabbing a chunk of steaming bread. "How did you sneak off with honey butter and fresh baked bread without Orla catching you?"

Efi shrugged. "She wasn't in the kitchens."

"Cac's! Any minute now we'll hear her shrill scream echoing through the forest, *Aoife*!" He chortled. His scouts chuckled in the background. It wasn't a normal day if you didn't hear the princess's name being screamed at least once by her godsmother and her face went red just thinking about it.

"Cil, I'm not cut out to be a princess. Orla's determined to tame the wild out of me. It simply won't happen. The nuance of court is lost on me too."

"This new life as royalty is something else entirely. Don't worry, you'll get there." he added.

"You're much better suited for the position than I am."

"I know Orla is trying to make you into the princess she thinks you need to be, but you don't need to change. You'll figure out how to navigate yourself soon enough. Time is all you require, and we have plenty."

"This is true. I did not think about it that way. I wish she thought like you do."

"Fret not sister, she will figure it out soon enough."

After their brief rest, Aoife and the company prepared to continue onward. They inspected saddle girths and harnesses before remounting their horses.

As they set off again, the narrow path gradually widened into a broad, well-worn road. Sunlight filtered through leafy branches arching overhead, dappling the riders with patches of light. Aoife gazed into the dense woods lining the road, glimpsing massive tree trunks and bushes laden with plump berries deeper within the forest's shade.

This region was a favorite grazing ground of the unicorns she knew. They feasted on the bountiful fruit and fresh greens thriving in hidden forest meadows. Their powerful magic sustained the wilderness in this part of Erainn. Which ensured both the abundance of the land and the security of their kingdom's eastern border.

Aoife decided she would visit her beloved unicorn friends after dealing with the strange plague ahead. For now, she urged Caisearbhan onward down the shaded road, keeping a steady pace. She tried to ignore the growing sense of unrest creeping into her heart, but the feeling continued to swell, spreading a chilling tendril of dread through her body.

She swallowed hard, fighting to master the escalating fear that was building within. But the eerie silence surrounding them ripped her breath away.

TWO

AOIFE

A Darkness in the Forest

THE STILLNESS OF THE FOREST FURTHER UNNERVED Aoife as they ventured deeper into the trees. No birds sang, no scurrying chipmunks rustled beneath the brush. Only their horses' hooves and harness bells pierced the eerie silence. The very leaves seemed to hold their breath as unease prickled Aoife's skin as she directed them further off the road. She glanced back at the scouts, their faces grave beneath helmet and hood. Then she led them into a small, sun-dappled clearing.

The scent of decay hit her first before she saw the trees—ashen, with cracked and peeling branches, as if someone had set them ablaze. Scattered across the withered grass were carcasses of birds, bats, and beasts.

Aoife froze, a growing horror rooting her in place. The once-vibrant wildflowers now drooped limply, their stems oozing a sickly reddish-black fluid that seeped into the soil. Where it touched, the earth looked scorched and barren, with a black substance crawling from the destruction—veining out from each lifeless shrub.

The soldiers shifted warily, mounts whickering and stamping. At Aoife's raised fist, they stilled. She dismounted on trembling legs, Caisearbhan's reins clutched tightly in her fist. Knees buckled as she sank to the ground. Plunging her hands into the dirt, she reeled from the trees' inaudible screams.

Cillian rushed over, crouching beside her. "Sister, breathe," he urged, gripping her shoulder.

Pulling free of the soil's torment, she focused on his voice through shuddering breaths. With Cillian's aid, she staggered upright on leaden limbs. But the pain in her hands remained.

When she beheld more animal carcasses spread out in droves across the decaying ground, reality shattered. She released a ragged scream; the sound torn from her soul. Squirrels, rabbits—even a badger—all lay slaughtered, their blood staining the meadow from one side to the next. How far did this terror spread?

Aoife took a struggling breath before speaking. "I have to fix this. Send your fastest back. We need as many healers as they can spare. Gather a small group of drakes to burn the bodies and trees. We must contain this immediately."

"Eamon." Cil called out.

The ranger next to Cillian's horse stepped his own steed forward. "Yes, your highness."

"You heard my sister. Ride hard and fast back to the palace. Bring every abled body to help cleanse the land."

"Straight away." Eamon clicked his teeth together and rode off back the way they came.

"Gods speed, my friend."

"Brother, I am worried," Efi said, "I cannot tell how far it goes. We'll need to dig down to find out, but let's wait for help to arrive. It's killing every flora and fauna it touches."

"Do you think the dark fae are responsible?" He asked.

"I'm unsure, brother. It didn't feel like fae magic at all. Something is terribly off. There are no magical energies lingering, just suffering and death. I've never experienced such pain. Besides us, I don't sense another fae presence here. I cannot tell what happened, but magic must be the answer."

"Then what do we do next?" Cil asked, brows furrowing.

"Whatever this is, it's spreading fast. We need to collect samples and take them back. Study them for answers. I am positive the alchemists and healers will be quick to sort this out."

"Don't be afraid to lean on me, sister. When father hears of this. I am sure he'll come to the border at once."

"No doubt he'll want to see this firsthand. Our lands rarely suffer like the human kingdom does, but *this* is unnatural. Will you scan the north area, then come find me?"

"Are you sure you want to go alone?" He asked her.

"Yes, I'll be all right, I promise. I need to focus. The kind that only comes with isolation. I might not feel residual magic here, but that doesn't mean I won't sense it elsewhere and I want little to no distractions. I know you understand."

Cillian nodded his head. She plodded along the border. The dirt path ahead showed more damage to Nairn's side than theirs. *I hold no love for humans, but they don't deserve this.*

The trees that lined it were black as night, their summer leaves shed to the ground. The disease spread across the soil, branching out like vines. Then it climbed up into the trees and shrubs, showing no mercy to anything within its grasp.

It seemed every plant had become infected. Luckily, she found no more bodies of birds or beasts as she kept walking. She hoped it meant that the other animals were actively avoiding the area. She scanned the area with her senses once more, hoping to detect the slightest evidence to determine who or what caused this. But then a shrill wail filled the space surrounding her.

Efi froze in her tracks. The summer air, once filled with warmth, went icy cold. Each tiny hair on the back of her arms stood erect. Her skin goose fleshed. A deep chill rippled through her spine. Her body jolted into action, and she ran toward the screams.

The cries echoed around her while her feet barely touched the ground. Like a small *Si Goaithe,* she whirled and weaved through the wooded area to the next clearing ahead. The sight of Onyx and Ivory colors made her heart sink to her knees.

Her dearest friend, the unicorn Nightwind, was in a state of panic as he hovered over his mate Dessa Astra. Her eyes locked on his muzzle, covered in a thick layer of sticky blood. He nudged his mate's face, then her side. He turned to Aoife. His silent, fearful gaze told her the situation was serious.

Several large gashes covered Dessa's body, including a bit mark on her neck. Blood oozed from them as Nightwind tried healing her with his horn. And with wounds like this, a unicorn's magic would cauterize them to stop the bleeding. *Why is she still bleeding then?*

"Oh, my gods No! Nightwind. What happened? She still bleeds." Efi sat down next to Dessa. Her hands outstretched over the poor horse's battered body. Nightwind's thoughts entered her mind. *My magic alone is not enough, princess. I cannot heal my love. I keep trying. Nothing is working. The cuts remain open.* His thoughts pierced her very soul and tugged deep at her heart.

"This isn't poison. Someone, something, did this to her. These teeth marks are unfamiliar. What did this to her?" She uttered before going straight to work.

I do not know. I went to drink from the nearby stream and found her like this. Whatever or whoever did this must be pure evil. Princess, will she live? Please say that you can save her. My magic, my healing, it's not working.

I will do what I can, my friend. I will fight with every fiber of my being to ensure she survives.

Aoife reached down and put her hands on her friend, "Hold on Dessa, I'm here with Nightwind. We'll heal you." A golden light flickered out of each of Aoife's fingertips and swirled down into Dessa's body with a gentle touch. A bit of light lingered, flickering throughout her mane with each shallow breath Dessa took in. But the wounds looked the same.

"Nightwind. I need your help." Tears streamed down Aoife's face. She glanced up, blinking them away, and stared deep into Nightwind's rich amber eyes. *Together, we can heal her.*

She wanted her words to start the healing process, but she feared they weren't enough. The light from her hands faded when uncertainty crept in. She took a deep breath, regaining her composure and continued to will her healing magic forth, hands suffused in a gentle glow. She put her palms over each wound and focused on the energy flowing from her fingertips into each torn sinew.

While nothing had completely healed up, the cuts looked better and had decreased in size. Her light pulsed brighter right as Nightwind's horn pushed into the massive wound on Dessa's ribs.

Muted groans escaped between Dessa's teeth. She was barely conscious. Nightwind's horn lit up Dessa's body with an intense glow. Efi joined the effort by providing a flood of healing energy for each cut. Gilded luminescence flowed between them and spread throughout Dessa, turning the color of her alabaster coat to a shimmering gold. The largest injury halfway closed up around the edges, but the center remained wide open. The smaller ones sealed off and entirely dissipated, leaving no marks to be seen. A sigh escaped Aoife's lips, carrying away the worries of almost losing her friend.

"Dessa, speak to me. Don't give up–fight for Nightwind, for me," Efi pleaded.

Dessa's head shifted a little, her chest rose and fell slightly with each shallow breath and Efi sensed the smallest exchange of words flow into her mind. *I will try.*

Aoife glanced at Nightwind giving him a gentle, reassuring smile. *In time, she will be fine.* Before the thought left her mind and entered his, the warm summer air turned biting cold. The bright sky darkened around them. And something unseen rushed right by and slammed into Aoife, flinging her into a nearby tree trunk. She hit the ground hard, dirt scrapping her cheek.

Nightwind reared with a piercing squeal, hooves pounding the earth. The force of it shook Aoife where she lay—stunned. Wincing, she touched her cheek, and her fingers came away bloody. *That's going to leave a mark.* She recognized the force she sensed watching her: *something powerful resides nearby, something familiar and fae-like.*

Her mind whirled, struggling to regain focus. Nightwind collapsed on his side, bright red blood flowed from a gash on his flank. She crawled on her stomach, writhing and squirming with frenzied, serpentine motions. Scraping desperately across pebbles and debris to reach him. She pressed her hands against it to stanch the bleeding. And began channeling her healing power into him.

Her stomach churned. It was all too much, but she persisted. She would not falter and had to save her friend. Before the cut sealed up, a second vicious blow struck her down, shocking her entire system. Scrambling to stand, Aoife clenched her fists.

“Make yourself known, fiend!” She screamed, getting back up on her feet.

Deep, maniacal laughter reverberated through the forest. The sound ricocheted off the trees before fading into the distance. Chest heaving, Aoife whirled and sprinted toward the lingering echoes, determined to confront whoever had hurt her friends. Her footsteps pounded swiftly through the underbrush, fury and adrenaline lending her speed.

The mocking voice still rang in her ears, fueling her rage. She skidded to a breathless halt by the weathered stone border, which marked the divide between Erainn and Nairn. All was tranquil and quiet now. Whatever evil had struck now vanished across the line.

Aoife stood poised at the boundary, its ancient

magic thrumming against her senses. She hesitated only a moment before reaching out her hand. Her fingertips grazed the invisible barrier, its power jolting through her body like a lightning strike. She recoiled, but determination blazed in her eyes.

Nightwind whinnied, calling her back to them. She took a quick look over her shoulder. *I can't let that thing hurt anyone else they'll understand.* She knew the repercussions of crossing without permission but didn't stop. She walked straight into Nairn without a second thought.

THREE

AOIFE

A Point of No Return

The chilling laughter continued as Aoife raced between the trees, using the sound to track her invisible foe. As she drew nearer, the voice rose to a booming crescendo, seeming to come from all around her.

"Oh, pretty princess, you can't catch me." It taunted her, the words dripping with malice.

"Watch me," she ground out, pushing her aching legs faster.

"I'd like to see you try," the voice purred before dissipating into silence.

An icy wave of fear washed over Aoife. Frozen in place, she strained to sense which way the creature had fled, but only the pounding of her heart filled her ears.

Without warning, a searing pain prickled along her skin. She gasped at the sudden hot breath hissing along the back of her neck. "I've marked you. Now I'll always be able to find you."

Efi spun around and grasped at the wisp of a shadow, but it melted away between her fingertips. Through blurred vision she saw it racing between the trees, deeper into Nairn. She had to pursue it before it could harm anyone else.

Aoife charged ahead, branches whipping against her face and tearing at her clothes. But she pushed on through the haze of fever that gripped her body. The taunting voice seemed to multiply, surrounding her as she ran.

Could there be more than one? The dire warnings of the Conclave whispered in her mind—perhaps the dark fae had finally come.

Aoife's hand flew to the burning pain on her neck. A swollen lump was forming where the creature had struck her. *What foul sorcery is this?* She needed a healer's skill, but Nightwind was too far away now. Could she risk turning back? *No, not now.*

Her stomach lurched violently, and she fell to her knees, retching. As she struggled for air, icy hands gripped her shoulders from behind. "Give up. You can't stop me," the sinister voice crooned. Cold fingers caressed her cheek. "My, my, aren't you beddable?" the wetness of its tongue skimmed across her jawline.

"Yes... I can," Aoife panted in defiance.

She staggered to her feet, squinting through the haze still clouding her sight. The creature was quick; she had to be quicker. Gritting her teeth, she pursued the flickering form deeper into the trees.

With each minute the fever spread, her body alternated between shivers and sweats. But she had trained to resist all manner of poisons—she would not falter. Up ahead, the murmured voice of the creature and two others echoed faintly. She honed in on the sound as the shadows converged.

The trees thinned out and revealed a sunlit glen. Through blurred vision Aoife made out three figures, their pointed ears marking them as fae. Insults filled the air on her approach. "*Dirty Faelyn. Unaligned whore*!" Beside them loomed the shadowed figure who pricked her. A large grin formed on their visible lips. Four sharp fangs and a long, pointed tongue protruded menacingly out from their mouth. She flinched when it licked one of the fae standing closest to it.

She watched in horror as it stretched out its long arm, touching a pine tree. The bark split open with a simple touch of a single pointed fingernail and black bubbled up and oozed out. *They're the ones responsible!* Filled with desperation, Aoife summoned her light magic and let the sun's warmth overwhelm her. She released it as a searing blast at her foes.

As they fell, she staggered forward, ready to drag one back for questioning. But at her feet lay two human children. Aoife collapsed in horror, gathering their small bodies in her shaking arms. Tears spilled down her cheeks. "No, no!" she cried. By the gods, had she hurt these innocent babes? No, these foul beings...

Their precious tiny faces with wild curls were still and unmoving, one red and one blonde. She touched their freckled round cheeks, her entire body shaking. Tears welled up in her eyes, her body trembled with fear. So young and small. She'd never hurt wee ones even if they were human.

"Oh Gods. What have I done? This is a trick of the poison. They can't be... It's a lie. Show yourself, you devil! I am not easily beguiled!"

Gloom swirled at the edges of Aoife's vision as the creature's sinister laughter echoed around her. "They will think it was you. Come with me now," it murmured from the encroaching shadows. A rugged arm stretched toward her from the inky black fog.

"Never!" Aoife spat in defiance, though her voice

quavered. Languor roiled within as she struggled to remain conscious.

What could she do? She had to heal the children, but her strength was rapidly fading. "Cillian!" she cried out in desperation. "Brother, I need you! Nightwind, help!"

But she knew no aid would reach her in time. Fighting down panic, she placed a trembling hand on each small body. Calling on the last shreds of her magic, she focused it into her glowing palms.

The golden light illuminated their sweet faces one last time before darkness rushed in. As unconsciousness took Aoife, a single question rang in her fading thoughts: Would her healing be enough? Then oblivion claimed her.

FOUR

AOIFE

What Have You Done?

Aoife drifted back to hazy semi-consciousness, cradled in her brother's arms. Cillian's angry voice filtered through the fog in her mind as he argued with a shadowy figure looming nearby. She tried to focus on the blurred silhouette, but a wave of discomfort washed over her. Instinctively, she nuzzled closer against Cillian's chest, seeking safety.

He gave her shoulder a gentle, reassuring squeeze as he lowered her to sit propped against a tree trunk. The stranger's voice rang out sharply, each word piercing Aoife's groggy mind like an arrow.

"Listen here tree focker I saw the witch and her devil's magic! She hurt my children!" She flinched.

Cillian's presence was the only thing keeping her panic at bay.

"Lies!" Cillian spat back, standing defiantly before them, shielding Aoife from the man's suspicious glares. She tried to rise, to explain, but her body felt weighted down with exhaustion. Her head lolled weakly against the rough bark.

"Nae! She was there, huddled over them with that weird light coming out of her hands. The Wolf King will hear about this treachery! You stinking pointy eared bastard!"

Cillian drew his sword and put the tip of his blade to the man's chest. "But you didn't witness her attack! Spit your lies one more time, human, and I'll cut you down where you stand!"

Two other humans, armed with axes, approached, siding with the man.

"It's true I heard screams then saw them laying still on the ground with her looming over them like the evil sorceress she is!"

Cillian turned to his scouts. "We need to leave now."

Efi groaned, "I didn't do this."

"Don't speak. We're going back to Erainn." he wrapped his arm around her.

She looked over at the two children being attended to by the first man who yelled at Cil. She forced herself out of her brother's grasp. "Please let me help them." She begged the man as she tugged at his sleeve.

He pushed her away. "Get your dirty fae hands off of them!" He scowled.

"But I am a healer. I was healing them, I swear. If I hurt them, their skin would be burned. It wasn't me, but others. Dark fae, I saw them. All of Nairn is danger if we don't stop them."

Cillian grabbed her arm and held on gently. "Efi, we need to go now."

"No, I can help, please!"

"I said get away. Our healers can deal with this." The man stood and steadily held up an enormous axe in both hands.

Cillian stepped between Aoife and the angry human, his broad frame shielding her protectively. "Return to your king," he commanded, his tone low and dangerous. "You don't want trouble here. Cross us, and you won't like what happens next."

To emphasize his point, her brother clamped down hard on the man's wrist with powerful fae strength. The human's axe wavered unsteadily in his grip, nearly tumbling from his hands.

The man winced, face reddening, but he held Cillian's unrelenting gaze. After a tense moment, the fight seemed to drain from the human's stance. He gave a reluctant nod, conceding this skirmish. Cillian released him and stepped back, folding his arms across his chest. The human glanced around uneasily as the rest of the fae scouts closed ranks behind their prince. They were clearly outmatched. The fae stood a head taller, with hardened muscles and ancient power shining in their eyes.

With a resigned scowl, the leader turned and stalked away with the children in tow; the others falling in behind him. Cillian tracked them until they disappeared from view, making certain they had retreated fully from where they stood. Once satisfied that the threat had passed, he turned back to tend to his sister.

"Shane, take her home to my father now. I'll check on the unicorns." Cil barked orders to the others, "The rest of you, come with me."

Aoife felt Shane's arm around her as he pulled her up onto his horse right in front of him. He held her tight and saluted Cillian.

"Brother, I–" She tried to speak as they rode off.

"Go! Before these fools change their minds." He said. Shane was quick to follow and whistled, sending his horse into a canter.

Tears trickled out of her eyes as they rode back to Erainn. On the way, Shane stopped to grab an important friend of hers—her horse, Cais. He slid out of the saddle with ease, leaving Aoife in the seat. He took Caisearbhan's reins, easing him forward before mounting his mare again.

"What have I done? My father will be so disappointed in me." She cried.

Shane slipped up on the saddle in front of her this time. "You're wrong, princess. I know you wouldn't hurt innocents. Now hold on tight."

"What if I did? That thing tricked me and the poison... it's possible. The man didn't tell me if their skin was burned, were they even breathing?" She felt sick again.

"Princess, they yet live. They will be fine. Your golden light lit up their bodies when we arrived, and I assure you I saw not a single burn." Shane tried to put her at ease, but she had her doubts.

"I hope you are right."

The scene was on repeat as they headed back to the palace. She failed to control herself again and now she couldn't avoid the consequences. *I should have stayed on our side, but what if...* She shuddered at the thought. Those dark fae had those children, and they had to be planning something way more nefarious than what happened.

She was unsure of what the future held. Would the Wolf King see reason where the woodsmen failed? Or was the peace they shared broken? As the silence enveloped her, she could hear nothing but the steady beat of hooves on the ground while her mind raced, and she feared the worst. If the humans wanted to fight, they would without hesitation. What would happen if the two kingdoms weren't united? *The worst possible.* The fae from her home realm would surely attack within a fortnight if they knew for sure that Nairn and Erainn were no longer allies.

Aoife couldn't shake the feeling that the daemon and dark fae she had seen were still lurking nearby. No doubt *infecting* more of Eavelaen. Nothing would stand in their way. The *Drothailte,* the barren wasteland of dark sands and twisted thorny bushes, separated the two kingdoms from other provinces that existed around the continent. And the door to Faery was buried deep in the thick of those thorns, but it was closer than the next ally if they could even secure one. The invasion would be devastating. *I can't let that happen.*

When they approached Ceannanas, the capital of Erainn, King Torin stood outside the great city with his guard. Ashamed for what she'd done, Aoife kept her head down, but her father took her up in his arms and held her close and she saw his eyes were red from tears.

"My little leaf. I have heard pieces of what

occurred. Tell me what happened, please." He ushered her back to the palace grounds.

"Of course, Father." She whispered, dragging one foot in front of the other.

A group of guards escorted them through the bustling streets. Her fae subjects unaware of what was happening. Life continued as if she hadn't done a thing. Plenty of the shopkeepers bade them hello. Her father greeted with them ease. Aoife didn't know how he could stay so calm. She remained silent with her thoughts of the whole situation swirling in madness. But tried her hardest to smile and acknowledge her people. *Have I failed them?*

"Shall we converse in the gardens? Near the Elder Tree?" Her father asked before they entered the gates to the palace.

"Yes, please," she breathed, her fingers twisting together anxiously.

Before she told him everything, beads of sweat gathered on her forehead. Her heart pounded beneath her chest and her body quivered. Her father's gentle demeanor calmed her nerves. His large hand rested on her shoulder. "You are safe here. You can tell me anything. I love you no matter what."

While she recanted all she had seen and heard, he listened intently. He didn't shout or condemn her, only took in each one of her words. Before he could speak, she blurted, "I'm so sorry, Da. I've really done it this time."

"We can get through this. Cullen is a good man, and he will see reason. You followed your heart, your deep intuition. I cannot say what is to come, but prepare yourself. Life in Erainn will forever change. Your path has also taken a different direction. One I have not foreseen."

"What do you mean? I thought he was the dreaded Wolf King?"

"Aye, they call him that because he is ruthless when he needs to be. Imagine being the first line of defense against the other warring kingdoms with a gateway to one realm sitting outside your border? Both kingdoms would be overrun if it wasn't for those mountains. His great-great-grandfather and me. We made a pact to always be allies, to be friends. Cullen will honor this promise as his forebears have done. I can assure you that."

"Are you positive? I crossed the line. One I cannot return unscathed from."

"Our fae kin will come by the thousands if we become enemies with the humans. We should focus on what needs to be said when we're called to justice on Nairn's side."

"Yes, I understand. What do I say?"

Her father's brow furrowed. "You tell the truth like

you've shared with me this day." He paused. "In the meantime, visit the gardens once a day. The rest of the time, you must stay in your rooms for your safety. Dark fae and humans might come after you. Let me see this mark on your neck before I take my leave."

"But Da..." She tried to protest, but the sternness in his eyes stopped her in her tracks. Aoife flipped her thick braid to the other side and her father inspected the bump.

"This is not dark fae. This is far worse... the mark of a daemon. Some call them the shadow fae from our home realm. The Light and Dark Courts would have you believe they are the only kingdoms within the realm of Faery, but deeper on the edges of the darkest borders lies the Shadow Court. This is... I must call the Conclave at once."

"I will join you." Aoife said.

"*No,* you will go to you room and *stay* there."

"Da, you're scaring me."

"Aoife, it appears as though you have committed several crimes. By oaths I made to Nairn, I must have you imprisoned until we convene with the Wolf King. Since you are the princess, this means your room will suffice. If we want Nairn to remain allies, you will do as I say, understood?"

"Yes, I'm sorry. I only wanted to help."

"Aoife, I don't fault you for chasing after that

daemon. Those creatures come from a far worse place than the Dark Fae courts. They live in the Shadowlands of Faery. Only a fool would dare make a pact with those daemons. I need time to go over this with the Conclave. For now, Orla will attend to you, and I will see you in two days' time. I will need to see this curse myself."

"What about Yseult?" She asked.

"Daughter. You've long made it clear you hate having someone tending to your daily needs. Orla will do as her godsmother duties demand. Nothing more. If you wish for Yseult to assist you for once. I will allow her to help you in the evenings, nothing more. I'll let you say goodbye to your friend here. The guards or Orla will fetch you shortly."

"Fair enough. Thank you da."

He hugged her tightly and left her sitting near the Elder Tree. The peacefulness of the tree washed over her. She replayed the scene in her head once more. *There had been two fae and the shadow being, err, the daemon. How did the children get there? Oh Creidhe Rootmother, why can't I recall what I saw? Lend me your serenity in the days to come. I'll miss the feel of your bark, the velvet of your leaves.* The tree responded not with words but images. Vivid flashbacks of their time spent flashed before her eyes. Aoife rested her head on the base and sighed.

The rootwalkers in the Eastern Forest showed me nothing but agony, and I heard their screams deep below the surface when my fingers were in the ground. What does it all mean? The hearty branches and trunk creaked and moaned. A small whisper graced the air with its presence. "I don't know. I have faith that you'll find out and stop this."

Aoife jolted up. It wasn't often that the Elder Tree spoke out loud. She was the mother of many trees around Erainn. She was the center of a network between them. If this curse spread, her dearest friend would be affected.

"I hope your faith is not misplaced."

The hurried sounds of feet on the stone pathways filled her ears, and she turned to see who they belonged to. Cillian appeared, bounding his way toward her. "Sister. I came to tell you that Nightwind and Dessa are alive and well." He sat down next to her, patting her hand.

"Are you up for company?" he asked.

She broke down into tears. "Of course! Thank you for tending to them," she squeaked.

Cil hugged her tight. He was the eldest by three minutes and the only sibling who had ever shown he cared for her. "Wait till the others hear about this... please keep our siblings at bay. I am not sure I can handle our younger brothers heckling me for this."

"Don't let them bother you. Brush off whatever they say. Bunch of ruffians and stumps, if you ask me." He grinned. "I don't think they'll nettle you about this. You protected both kingdoms today, sister. Those humans haven't a clue what you saved them from."

"Hels, neither do we... well, Da seems to know, but he didn't tell me a lot about them and the Shadowlands in Faery," Aoife sighed. Her head drooping in disappointment. She lifted her gaze to look at her twin brother wistfully. "Wish he had."

"Aye, that would have been helpful. Da mentioned something worse than a dark fae to me. Like a daemon? You said it had four fangs? Didn't realize they came from Faery, did you?" he asked.

"That took me by surprise. What else do we not know about? What's the difference between a daemon and fae, if any? I guess our elders were right. Our enemies are out there. Bitter about our freedom. Wanting to tear us down."

Cil moved to stand before her. His hands firmly gripping her shoulders. "They fear change Efi. Like right now, fear sits with you. Let it go and whatever happens, happens, know it is a fate we are hurdling toward."

His voice took on a soothing tone. "All will work out, that's what I feel. You didn't hurt those children, I know it." He gave her shoulders a reassuring squeeze, holding her gaze steadily.

"I hope you're right, brother. I'm worried that the worst may come. They pricked me in the neck with something, too. Whoever that daemon was... they said they'd always be able to find me. What if... What happens next? Will I be prepared?"

Drawing back, Cil stroked his chin, his eyes narrowing intently as he pondered the situation. "Even here, while we sit with unknowns. A force pushes us in the right direction, sister. I sense it deep in my bones. Have some faith and maybe a little good will come of this?"

"Like what?"

"We will have to wait and see. Don't let anyone stop you from being who and what you are."

"I won't brother." She reached out and squeezed his arm.

"Good."

The whisper of slippers on stone echoed into Aoife's ears. Someone was approaching. Getting up, she careened to the side and saw Orla hurrying toward them, face pinched with concern. With a flap of her hands, she shooed Cillian away before grasping Aoife's shoulders, steering her back to her chamber. Inside, Yseult greeted Aoife with an eager smile, clearly bursting to share the latest palace gossip. She sat Aoife down and began brushing her long tresses, chattering away animatedly about the latest gossip: Lady Cliona had taken three mortal lovers in one night and wasn't even trying to hide anymore.

"Thank you, princess. I'm so happy you asked me to attend to you this evening. I can barely believe the rumors of Lady Cliona, can you?"

"No. Thank you for being here. You shouldn't have to help me, but I am glad to have your company. Cliona has no shame. She belonged to the Dark Court in Faery. It's not uncommon for them to take multiple lovers. Though my father would find it a practice best left there, I see no issue with it if everyone consents and is happy, so why not?" Aoife winked, and turned to Yseult, "I miss our lessons with Miren, and our time spent baking in the kitchens, don't you?"

"Oh, but you're the princess now. Proper and all that... I miss them too, Efi—your highness." She corrected herself.

"I am simply fae, like you, nothing more. We are all equals." She grimaced in the mirror, and Yseult kept quiet, her fingers deftly working up loose night braids for her to sleep in.

"Thank you for considering me as an equal." Yseult's voice was timid as she crossed one piece of hair over another.

"Yseult, please, you need to recognize that even

with our status, my father also believes in equality for all. We do this to blend in with other kingdoms. We will never stoop low as the humans do with our proposed servants."

"Of course, your highness, thank you again."

Efi reflected on a time when her father hadn't been a king, but when the Conclave rose her family above their station everything changed. All because her father secured an iron-clad alliance with the humans that had lasted over one hundred years. He had also marked the land they lived on as the Unaligned Kingdom of Erainn.

She still didn't understand why, after two hundred years, they needed a king. Before it was just the Conclave leading. She stopped her friend and looked her deep in the eyes. "Thank you for dealing with me as I accept these changes in my life."

Yseult bowed her head low. "For you, I'd do anything. You truly are one of the strongest fae I have met. We are blessed to have you as our princess."

"Your words are incredibly kind. I am committed to doing my best for Erainn, but I am far from perfect. Which is made obvious by the circumstance I find myself in."

"I'll pray to Faerayen for your cleared name and safe return home from Nairn." Yseult bowed her head in a short prayer, her eyes closing. Aoife did the same, remaining silent until she heard her say: ahaneevewyven.

"Thank you," she whispered.

Aoife was grateful for Yseult's cheerful assistance and companionship over the next few days. As Yseult prepared to leave for the evening, Aoife embraced her tightly.

"I am grateful for you," she softly uttered. Yseult gave her a gentle, reassuring squeeze before departing.

Alone, Aoife wandered to the open window and breathed in the cool night air. It soothed her troubled thoughts. Below, hundreds of fireflies gleamed in the gardens, flickering like candlelight as they danced through the flowers. Their carefree motion was at odds with the unease in her heart.

She leaned against the stone sill, hugging her shawl close against the breeze. Irreversible change was on the horizon. Her old life vanished like smoke; a new, uncertain path lay ahead. She gazed up at the vast expanse of stars, constellations she'd known since childhood, and suddenly felt small and lost. A silent tear slipped down her cheek. While the others hoped she'd be free to return, she couldn't help but feel she wouldn't, and if she did. Nothing would be the same as it had been.

FIVE

AOIFE

Given to the Wolf King

Aoife roamed back and forth, fiddling with her necklace, eyes darting about as she retraced nervous steps around the perimeter of her chamber. The swish of her skirts whispered rhythmically in tune with her slippered footsteps. Only an hour remained before they departed with her father's guard. Orla had quietly informed her that King Cullen would meet their party at the border.

She wrung her hands, dreading the journey ahead. She would travel to Nairn a second time, praying they would see reason. The woodcutter would be there too. Aoife shuddered, unsure how she would withstand his accusatory glare.

'Don't let your temper rule you this time,' Orla had warned. Aoife sighed, hoping she could restrain her fiery tongue when it mattered most.

A heavy knock broke her from her thoughts. Her younger twin brothers, Rowan and Eoghan, cracked the door open and filed in. Their playful spirits absent from the beginning of their arrival. They were unnaturally solemn and taciturn. Their changed demeanor amplified Aoife's growing unease.

She realized her father had not disclosed everything about this meeting with King Cullen. Rowan fidgeted anxiously, while Eoghan simply stared, his normally laughing eyes now grave and troubled. Rowan pulled Aoife into an uncharacteristically fierce embrace before murmuring awkward well wishes.

"Efi, fear not. Faerayen is with you this day." Rowan said.

"I hope so."

"We will see you again. I'm sure of it." He replied, but Eoghan remained silent and statuesque.

A knot formed in the pit of Aoife's stomach. Though her father insisted King Cullen was an honorable man, he was still human. Some mortals viewed the fae with suspicion and contempt. What if she was being led into a trap? Or worse? *Death.*

She pushed the dark thought away and lifted her

chin. Whatever the morn held, she would face it with courage and integrity.

Orla burst into her room with a soft pink gown draped over her arms. "Rowan and Eoghan, pleasure to see you both this morning. I need to get your sister ready now, so you'll need to leave."

"Yes, mam." Rowan said before he kissed the top of Efi's head and left.

Eoghan hung around. His silence persisted. He gathered her up in his arms in the tightest hug she ever had from him. "Please come back to us from Nairn. I don't know what I'd do without you," he whispered.

"I will." Aoife assured him, though an uneasy prickle crept up her spine. Eoghan was gifted with prophetic dreams, and he must have glimpsed some troubling vision of her fate. Why else would he hold his silence, sharing nothing beyond this cryptic farewell? Eoghan never spoke of his dreams until their meaning became clear.

She studied her brother's somber face, searching for any glimmer of insight. But his expression remained closed, his thoughts a mystery. She swallowed back the flood of questions on her tongue. When the time was right, Eoghan would tell her what he knew. Until then, she could only trust that the answers would come in their own hour.

There were some magics even the fae could not rush.

"I know Rowan and I tease you too much. For that, I am sorry. You were there to care for us when mother died. In ways, you are a mother to us, and we are grateful even if we don't tell you oft enough as we should. I love you sister."

Before his hand met the doorknob, she grasped onto his fingers and asked him if he had a dream. He gulped, then sighed. A slow nod came next. She acknowledged him mentally. *Please tell me more when you can piece the dreams together more coherently.* His words filled her mind. *I will.*

I love you too, brother. I'll return soon, you'll see. Her gaze followed him out the door before he closed it. She turned around bleary-eyed and shuffled back to her godsmother.

Orla fumbled through the vanity drawer for a hairbrush. "Time for us to prepare, my dear. I gave Yseult the day off. I'll fix your hair today."

Efi frowned. "Did you have to choose pink?"

Orla huffed, "You bet I did! You need a color that makes you appear innocent! I don't trust these humans. You'll want to appeal to their senses in more ways than one! Soft pink will ease their anger and give you an air of sweetness. As long as you keep yourself under control."

Efi pressed her lips together, "I'm not that hot-headed Ma... I suppose you have a point with the pink though, but I'd much rather wear the green one. Please?"

"No arguing with me. You need all the help you can take."

She conceded. "Fine, I understand."

After picking at the frilly thing from Orla, she slid behind her divider to put the ensemble on. She pulled it over her undergarments and fixed the sleeves.

From behind the dividers, she stepped out, glanced in the mirror. *Hmm, I don't hate it.* And sat down. Her godsmother approached and gently brushed her rich, golden mahogany blonde hair. Her deep forest green eyes stared back at her from the mirror. She brushed her cheeks with a simple peach rouge and applied rose balm to her lips.

Orla pulled a pearl circlet out of the drawers and worked up two small braids around her head before setting it in place and soothing out the unruly waves that fell over Aoife's shoulders.

"All set." Orla's voice was grim.

"No one will say it to my face. Speak plainly to me. There is fear in your eyes. My father and my brothers' too. They are not their usual selves. You're worried about what will happen in Nairn."

"Ta, but your father assures me that this Cullen

will see reason. Some humans still hold hate for the fair folk. They forget *we* left. We made a choice. To change. Let us hope they see this. Now off to the courtyard entrance to meet our carriage."

"Yes, Mam."

The two of them headed out front where her father and Cillian were waiting. Cillian took Efi by the arm and helped her up into her seat. Orla soon followed, and off they went. The ride was uneventful, and the two hours passed quickly.

When the door to their carriage opened, she was met by a group of humans already waiting at the meeting place. She hesitated but got out. There were hushed gasps from the crowd. Efi looked to her right. Her people had shown up in full force.

The sight of all of them made her heart swell, and she smiled at them. She was grateful for their presence. It helped her feel strong. She could face what came next, but she saw *him*—the woodsman and her knees buckled.

Next to him stood a man far taller than any human or fae there. Bright blue eyes immediately caught Aoife's attention, contrasting against the man's golden beard and cropped blonde mane. His hair was an unruly mass of thick waves, trimmed short around the ears, with longer strands falling across his face, a small scar cut through his left brow. Wide shoulders and muscular arms, far more imposing than any fae she'd seen. He had muscles that no fae man would ever possess. She found she could not look away, surprised by his striking visage. Everything about him drew her in. *For being human... he's quite something to behold.*

Was he the legendary Wolf King she had heard about? The thought quickened her pulses. She studied him openly, noting the way he carried himself. The keen intelligence in those piercing steeled eyes. What mysteries might lie behind such a striking personage? What was he truly like beneath the hardened exterior?

Aoife nearly laughed at her own fanciful musings. There were more pressing matters at hand than gawking at handsome strangers.

A reedy, unpleasant looking fellow stepped forward then, breaking the spell the blonde man's presence had cast over her. He hailed her father as their party dismounted.

"Hail there, fae king," the man greeted them with an oily voice that slithered like a serpent.

Aoife eyed him closely. This human, whoever he was, seemed cunning and sly. She would not trust him easily.

"King Cullen thanks you for your prompt attention to this matter and appreciates your timeliness," the thin man continued.

Aoife bristled at his presumptuous tone, as if her father were the one who should be grateful. She willed her temper to cool, reminding herself that diplomacy must rule the day.

"Thank you, Nat. I can take it from here." The man with the blue eyes stepped forward. *He is the Wolf King*. Aoife's breath caught as his gaze fixated on her, stirring unfamiliar sensations that fluttered within. What was this inexplicable pull she felt towards this man?

Aoife inhaled sharply, lifting her chin to meet his intense stare. Her heart hammered against her ribs. Unconsciously, she brushed her fingertips along her forearm, edging closer, though she knew not why.

Cullen's eyes slowly roamed over her, a small smile tugging at the corner of his mouth before meeting her view again.

Their gazes held, the cacophony of the crowds fading to a low hum. For a suspended moment, no one else existed: only the two of them bound in wordless connection. Awareness arced between them like lightning. The air thickened until Aoife could scarcely draw breath.

Cullen's eyebrow ticked upward, a glimmer of something dangerous in his cobalt eyes. Before Aoife could grasp the meaning, their focus shattered as more humans approached.

"King Cullen, I haven't seen you since you were twenty. With that beard, I thought you were old king Weylan. How *is* your father doing?" King Torin spoke.

He strolled over to her father and brushed right past, grazing her arm with his, leaving her breathless.

She turned her head to glance back at her father, who was standing behind her, and watched the two kings greet each other like brothers. Nat pulled himself back into the crowd after she glimpsed him out of the corner of her eye. She swore his eyes were on her the entire time, but didn't want him to notice she was aware.

"Sadly, he is unchanged. I dare say, shall we begin? Torin, my old friend?" The Wolf King asked her father.

"We shall. We can discuss your da another day. Where is the witness? Brogan the woodsman, correct?"

"Here." The woodcutter stepped forward and recounted what he witnessed. She wished he had caught sight of the dark fae. He made it sound like she was evil. Her skin crawled at his accusations.

The man's lies were met with a fierce response from the fae crowd, who shouted and grew increasingly disruptive. Pushing their way toward him in a flurry of green, gold, and silver hues. Cillian and the guards tried to calm them down.

Each side threw insults around. "The human lies. You fool-hardy mortals know nothing of real magic if it shot you in the eye." A fae onlooker mocked the humans.

"Knife eared leaf lickers!" yelled one human in the middle of the crowd.

"Filthy upright, talking swine!" Retaliated someone on the fae side.

"Shut yer puss ya tree humper."

"You first! Oink! Oink!"

Aoife stepped forward and bade her people to quiet down. The crowd fell silent. She felt Orla's hand touch her back. A reminder to stay quiet, to stay calm. She sighed and looked around. She was next.

"And what does the accused have to say?" King Cullen questioned.

Aoife cleared her throat, looked at her father, who nodded. She told her side of the story. Orla's hand stayed firm in place. Everyone calmed down and listened to her every word.

"And then the children were lying there. It was irresponsible of me to throw fae magic around when I knew it had poisoned me, but that creature, that being, is still out there and no one is safe until we take it down."

She watched as the Wolf King deliberated. His eyes studied hers, and her heart skipped a beat. He was deciding her fate, and all she could do was take in his handsome face. *I should not feel attracted to the man who holds my life in his hands.* It was an odd sensation, and his stare only became more intense. She rubbed her fingers against her palms. How would she feel when he judged her? Her feelings were already confusing her.

Nat slid next to the king and whispered in his ear. No doubt he wanted the worst to occur. She could see it in his sickly yellowed eyes as he took a small peek at her. *He hates me, though he doesn't know me. Father was right, hatred doesn't help anyone. Please forgive me, Lilithann, for I have done the same.*

King Cullen spoke. "I have heard both sides, yet we are still missing all the details. The infected forest clearly points to dark fae and not the unaligned, but this fae woman here crossed borders without proper permission. She also carelessly threw about her magic. Things could have gone much worse. She needs to make restitution either way."

"Ta, I agree Cullen and as her king I plan to have my citizen do just that," Torin said at last.

"But my liege. Those children may not survive the night!" Nat slipped in.

Brogan piped up, "Sire. They were stable before I left, and she was right. Their bodies have no burns. I saw her golden fingertips when I arrived. Maybe I have let emotion rule my actions since, but they are my children, they are my life."

"So, she heads to the Taithe to heal them right away," King Cullen replied.

"If they don't make it. I say she dies along with them! Who's to say she's not playing both sides? She could have made a deal with her fae kin. We'd never know," Nat demanded.

Torin scoffed. "King Cullen. Aoife is one of our healers and takes care of the forests. What he suggests is mere conjecture and lies. She rushed in without thinking. This doesn't make her a traitor, and she's certainly not dark fae."

"I am inclined to agree with you, Torin. Still, this matter is delicate..." Cullen paused.

The human crowd had been silent up to this point, but she heard some of them agree with that snake of a man. Not a second later, a fight broke out. Eamon and Shane had jumped some men and their friends were swift to follow. More fae and humans started throwing fists right away.

"That. Is. Enough!" King Cullen roared, his voice morphing into a thunderous howl that seemed more wolf than man. He stepped between the two sides, exuding a palpable aura of dominance. All stilled at his command, the weight of unspoken power behind his chilling stance. Even the slippery man, Nat, cowered and slunk backward, properly cowed into silence.

Aoife released a shaky breath, pulse hammering from the sheer force of Cullen's presence. He seemed to be no ordinary human; an ancient wildness lived within him. She had witnessed nothing like this before.

A shiver danced down her spine, though she did not know if it was born of fear or fascination. Perhaps both. One thing was certain: King Cullen was not a man to trifle with. She felt a flicker of gratitude that his fury was not directed at her.

"King Torin and I will discuss this matter further *alone* since we are amongst children. I'll have you all remember that the people of Erainn are on our side. Even this woman we judge now *is not* our true foe. Dark fae cannot harness the sun's magic like this one. Even the woodcutter has said her magic was bright as the sun. We need to work together to heal both lands faster to keep the Courts of Faery at bay."

Lowered voices filled the crowds, but muffled words resounded loud enough for her to hear.

"Kill her now and be done with this mess. You can't trust the Fae."

"Stupid humans and wanting to kill things they don't understand! Say it my face, you cowards if you dare." Shane threw his fists in the air then drew his sword, ready to take on any human that stood in his way.

"The unaligned fae are on our side!" a human woman stomped her foot to the ground and braved the fae haters by Shane's side. More humans joined them, and tears welled in Aoife's eyes. *They don't know me, they don't know us, but they stand with us all the same.*

Cil, of course, pulled him back and bade him to put his sword away.

Her father stepped forward. His voice just as commanding as Cullen's. "When the rest of you can act accordingly, we might consider your points. For now, the kings will decide from here on out."

No one interjected after his pronouncement. It was the law of both lands. The two kings stepped away, conferring in hushed tones before they entered a private grove of trees near the meeting place. A solid hour passed before they came back and by then she was shaking from head to toe.

When they returned, her father spoke, his voice booming over the droves of people waiting for an answer. "This is our decree. Aoife, citizen of Erainn. You are now a ward to the King of Nairn. You will remain in good faith to make recompense for trespassing and recklessly casting magic in an unsafe manner. To ensure the bond holds fast, you will first heal the afflicted children. You will work alongside

Nairn to halt the spreading taint in their lands and stay until their king releases you from this duty."

Efi's jaw dropped, shock freezing, her body in place. *A mere citizen? And a ward? Why lie? I'm the princess of Erainn.* This meant nothing less than being a prisoner in her mind. How could her father allow such a thing?

"Our kingdoms cannot thrive alone. Only together as allies are we strongest," Cullen said.

"Unless you want the host of the Fae Realm set upon us all. They'll spare no one in their bid to take over. Destroying both kingdoms until it is a barren wasteland," her father added gravely.

"Aye! King Torin speaks true!" Cullen affirmed. "This is our final word on the matter. Citizens of Nairn, return to your homes, but keep watch, so we may continue in peace. Report anything out of the ordinary to my guards at once."

"People of Erainn, do the same," her father commanded.

Both human and fae crowds stood in stunned silence. Most seemed to grasp that this alliance protected all and began drifting away in small groups.

She noted Nat's clenched jaw as he held his tongue, grumbling under his breath and throwing his hands up before storming off toward the other humans. Soon, the remaining fae melted away as well until the area was devoid of the throngs that once stood there. Only the kings, their guards, and the woodcutter. He slowly approached her and said a soft hello and it startled her.

"Aoife. I wish I knew what happened. I don't know if yer lying to save your own skin or you were in the wrong place at the wrong time, but our healers can't fix my children. If you can save them, miss. You have my thanks and forgiveness. I had time to calm down and talk this over with our king. He's a wise man, a learned man, unlike myself. I trust him and his decisions."

"Of course I'll heal your children. I hope we are leaving right away to attend to them. The sooner the better, as I have no idea what those dark fae did to them."

"Thank ya miss" he went to put his hand out to shake hers and she took it in hers. Right as they shook, Nat appeared out of nowhere and strolled over to them.

A smug smirk hung on his face, which made Aoife roll her eyes in annoyance.

"Ah, Aoife was it? You came by the king's carriage? Do the fae hold each other as equals at court? Usually, such escorts are oft for a high-ranking lady, but you are so young and a simple healer." He grabbed her hand to kiss it, but before his lips touched her skin, Orla smacked it away.

"You mind yours, you slippery *little man,*" she huffed.

"Orla, where's your etiquette today?" King Torin approached.

"I'll mind mine, if he does the same." She glared up at her king.

"Orla," he chided her.

"Torin," she retorted.

It was obvious from the look in their eyes that words unspoken passed between them.

Her father turned to him. "Nat. Are you part of the king's court?" he asked, trying to draw attention away from her godsmother.

"Yes, Nathair please. I was on Whelan's close counsel, but our strong-willed Cullen prefers to confide in his peers." He clicked his teeth. His tone dripping with disgust.

"Can't imagine why. The way you slither about like a serpent, no doubt." Orla locked eyes on him.

Efi observed them both as they stared each other down. Orla's face darkened while Nathair shrunk down at her gaze.

"Enough," King Cullen interceded. "It appears we both have hard-headed individuals as part of our court. Lady Orla, is it? And this is Aoife? Esteemed members of your conclave?"

"Yes, you are correct," Torin answered. A wash of relief spread across his face. *They are both hiding that I am the princess. I don't understand.*

He respectfully took her hand in his and bowed his head. "You can take your leave, Nat. I can handle everything from here."

"Yes, sire, of course. I meant no offense." He bowed right as a black carriage rolled up behind him.

His shoulders slumped before he climbed in. Efi was glad to be rid of him and his dark fae-like aura. *I bet King Cullen sees right through him.*

Orla muttered under her breath, "Good riddance. He was tainting the air."

"Orla..." Torin's eyes widened.

King Cullen smirked and nodded in silence before speaking up. "Aye, lady Orla is right, but let's move on. We'll head to Bearsden at once."

He whistled in a high pitch tone and a tall knight came running to his side.

"This is Dylan. My right hand. He will accompany Brogan and Aoife to the Taithe. I will lead the wagons there. We'll head for my castle if time permits. If not, we'll rest for the night and return to Falkirth at first day's light."

"I am ready and so is Aoife." Orla gathered up her skirts.

"Orla, you're not going with them." King Torin stopped her in her tracks.

"By the shadowed fae! What! Torin. Surely..." she spoke, flabbergasted.

"Aoife will go alone."

"I think not! You'd send your only daughter with these brutes? Shame on you Torin. You'd take my godschild away? Maeve's spirit will surely haunt you for this! You forget oaths made long before this one."

The mention of her mother's name made Aoife more apprehensive.

"Is there something the matter?" King Cullen asked.

"Yes, you two bull-headed men sorted this out and forbade Aoife's godsmother to come with! I doubt king Torin told you what my promise means!" Orla snapped.

"Lady of the waters, queen of the deep. Please Orla. This is how it needs to be." He took up her hands and held them in his. Pleading with her to accept the terms the two kings had agreed upon.

"I won't stand for this. Strike me down if you must, but I will not leave her side."

"Orla," Torin sighed, "You know the word of the king is the last word, stop arguing and listen to me."

Cullen cut in. "Torin, if this woman insists. She can come later. But for now, Aoife must come alone. I won't mention who she is, and I promise she is safe with me, but if we bring Orla with us, they might suspect that Aoife is more than we claimed."

"Of course, Cullen. I will see that Orla holds her tongue and takes a step back."

Orla glowered at them, eyes sparking. "Her *safety?* You think your daughter is safe with that beast of man? Oh, you men and your... I can't stand to look at any of you!" she cried, throwing her hands up in disgust. She whirled around, storming off toward the carriage with her skirts swirling violently around her legs. After a few paces, Orla spun on her heel to pace back, grumbling angrily under her breath staring at King Torin.

Aoife didn't envy her father one bit. He'd have to tame her godsmother's rage later on his own. A small grin formed on her lips. *And she calls me short-tempered. I will miss her.*

The Wolf King approached her next. "Lady Aoife, Dylan will escort you to the wagon now. If you are ready. Follow us this way." Cullen offered her his hand, and she took it, but turned to face her da.

"F-father, is this what you want me to do?"

"Aoife, you crossed the border illegally and acted recklessly. Learn from this, and perhaps learn more about our human allies. We must stop the hatred growing between our kinds. For the good of all, we cannot afford the freedoms our people enjoy. Sacrifices are required on our end. Cullen, I hope you understand what I am entrusting you with."

"I do, sir. As the only heir to Nairn's throne, a lot has fallen on me since my father's illness took hold. I will always uphold my word to you, Torin. Our actions right now matter, shaping the security of both kingdoms in the months to come."

"How is Good King Whelan, by the way? Does his sickness still plague him? Aoife is the best healer in all of Erainn. I am sure she can assist in his treatments," Torin said.

Cullen sighed gravely. "He yet lives, but the illness has taken firm root. I have reigned in his stead these five long years. You have my thanks again, Torin. We shall endure this trial together. In a month's time, I will send a trusted messenger to update you on our progress."

Torin turned to Aoife. "Come, we must say goodbye." He reached for her, but she shrank from his touch.

"I never thought it would come to this. How long must I be gone?" she cried.

Torin's eyes were sad but resolute. "For as long as King Cullen decrees. Prove yourself trustworthy, and we will secure your role as emissary, then home you can return."

Aoife shook her head vehemently. "Father, how can you expect me to accept this? I beg you, do not force this fate upon me!"

Her father would not relent. "The decision is final. Break this pact, and you endanger yourself and our alliance. Do this for Erainn, for your people."

Resigned, she whispered, "You leave me no choice. I'll go. At least let me say my goodbyes to Ma and Cil."

"Cillian, embrace your sister now. Orla, you as well," Torin urged.

Aoife clung to them, holding back bitter tears. They huddled together; arms wrapped around each other. Every second with them, she savored as it felt like it would be her last.

When she turned to her father, his outstretched arms met only her cold rejection. Hurt filled his eyes, but she looked away and marched to the wagon as the guard Dylan tried to help her up, but she batted his hand away and climbed in alone. She kept her chin up and didn't look back. Dylan climbed in after and sat across from her, then shut the door. She felt the carriage jolt forward, carrying her off unwillingly toward the unknown.

SIX

AOIFE

Face to Face

SHE STARED DOWN AT HER FEET AS THE CARRIAGE rattled along towards the Taithe, some sort of human healing hut by her understanding. What would await her there? What it would be like? Perhaps crossing the border had been a mistake after all. *There is something to be said about the lesson of thinking before doing. My actions have led me here. Now I must face the consequences.*

Aoife hoped she could withstand what trials came next. The hatred she felt during her trial was intense. At least there she had her people behind her. Here, she had no one to confide in. *I can't believe my father stopped Orla from coming with me. I need her now more than ever*. Without warning, the carriage came to an abrupt halt, jarring her from her thoughts.

Dylan flung open the door and yanked on her arm without a word, trying to escort her out. The entire ride he had stayed silent, a scowl across his face, and now he was forcing her out of the wagon like she wasn't a ward but a prisoner like she first assumed. *Are these humans really allies or are they enemies?*

"Excuse me? Take your hands off me." She shoved his hands away. "I can get out myself if you're going to be so rough with me."

She pressed past him and hopped down from the step by herself. Cullen chuckled and smacked his guard on the back. "Better be careful with that one, my friend. She's spitfire."

Dylan grumbled under his breath, and Aoife shot him a withering glare. "Where do we go from here, *King* Cullen?" she asked.

"That large building just ahead." Cullen pointed to a sprawling wooden structure down a muddied path.

Aoife grimaced. "Is there no other way?"

"No, lady Aoife," Cullen replied, offering his hand.

She eyed the mud, dread building inside her. Thinking of the gown she wore, she cringed: Orla would have a fit if she knew Efi was about to drag the dress through the muck.

"Come now, afraid to get a little dirty?" He teased.

"Oh, no King Cullen. I am afraid of what will happen when Orla sees the gown again," Aoife admitted, digging her teeth into her lip.

Cullen laughed. "I can't say I blame you there. Though our encounter was brief, she's a force to be reckoned with. I don't envy your father one bit."

"You have no idea, your highness."

Before he could assist, Aoife gathered up her skirts and took off in a sprint. The tips of her toes barely touched the ground as she blazed ahead. Leaving the men behind, their mouths gapping.

There was a sense of suspicion radiating among the townsfolk as they eyed her carefully. Their eyebrows crooked up with concern when she raced past them. Her hair flowed wildly behind her, exposing the point of each ear. One lady gasped. The word *fae* touched Aoife's ears in a faint whisper. The woman then shooed her children into a small hut next to a blacksmith's workshop as she shot by.

Efi paid no mind. Her only goal was to ensure the gown remained unstained. She'd rather face the scrutiny of the people from Bearsden over Orla any day. She made it to the door of the healer's hut before anyone else. Using the edge of the steps, she scrapped caked mud off her shoes and let her dress plunge to the ground once she reached the doorway. She waited for her escorts to arrive and looked back down the street to find them.

Cullen was close behind her, Dylan huffed, trailing behind him, his armor jangling while he muttered under his breath about how difficult he had it trying to guard both now, and the king boomed with laughter. Once they reached the entrance, she stepped to the side and Dylan slung the door wide and ushered them inside.

Aoife walked into the dim interior of the Taithe. The stench within assaulted her senses. The overpowering smell of festering wounds, sickness, and decay permeated the air. She gagged, hastily covering her nose and mouth with her hand.

Her eyes watered as she scanned the space next. The sour odor of sweat and bodily waste mingled with bitter tonics. Across the room, a heap of bloodied bandages sat out in the open while a harried healer ground up poultices unaware of the reek surrounding him.

Aoife steeled herself and swallowed down the nausea settling into her stomach.

"Aye, what's this about?" a wiry white-haired fellow bellowed out from farther back in the room.

"Hew, you old geezer, do you not recognize your own king?" Dylan said.

"Of course, lad, ya think I'm daft. I'm talkin' about her with her nose all turned up."

"Ah, she's fae, that's why. I don't think they're accustomed to the smell of human disease and death."

"Well, bring her here and I'll show her to the children," he motioned for them to follow.

Efi hesitated and the old man swung back around. "Come on, girl! You don't have the time to spare, now do ya?" He directed her to come with him again, this time guiding her forward.

She shook her head and got in line behind him. They proceeded down a lengthy hallway, passing six doors. She kept track of them all. Memorizing everything she saw. When they came up to the room on the left. Hew propped opened the door and there were the two children laying in beds butted up against each other.

"They're twins. Before they fell asleep again, they begged to be next to each other. I think it did them some good, been stable ever since," he said.

"Absolutely it did." She whispered, dashing over to them as fast as she could.

She gazed upon the children. Their curly hair had a life of its own—Wild and untamed, contrasting their low energy and pallid faces. Their freckled cheeks drained of their rosy sheen she remembered seeing days earlier. She touched each face softly and pressed her hand on their foreheads. They were hot to the touch. Each breath they took shallower than the one before.

Taking one hand from each, she focused on the souls within their bodies. "Oh, little ones," she whispered, her face twisted up with pain.

Hew came over with a box full of tools she'd never seen before, then pulled up a stool next to her. "I haven't the faintest how fae heal, so tell me what ya need, and I'll gather up the supplies for you. Here's a box of our usual implements,"

"I need nothing but my hands." She said.

"Like the druid? I suppose you haven't met him yet though, so you wouldn't know now, would ya?"

The old human seemed like a strange fellow, so Efi simply agreed and worked her light up and sent it into the hearts of the two children.

Hew's eyes got big. "That's nothin' like the Druid. What manner of sorcery is this?"

"Healing light."

She could hear Brogan, the woodsman, and the king talking behind them. He was worried about her magic not healing them. Efi stopped and turned to look at them. She promptly got up and inspected the woodcutter's limbs. He had a large bruise and a cut on his forearm.

She cupped her hands around the injuries and

inhaled deep before releasing it. "What are you do–" she shushed him before he could speak and held his arm tight in her hands while her fingers lit up.

He squirmed a little at first. His gaze flicked back and forth between her face and his arm. The bruise dissolved, and the cut sealed up. Within seconds, the wound disappeared. Fresh new skin in its place.

"Wow!" He exclaimed.

She turned around and started working on the children again. The men attempted to speak, but she silenced them with a hush and cleared her throat before continuing. But the king edged closer to her, like he was testing her abilities, and she felt his eyes on her backside. Those strange new feelings she had earlier crept in once more. An unwelcome distraction with her trying to heal the children.

The light from her hands grew dull as she lost concentration. "Please scoot back," she told him, but he didn't move.

She spun around, finding him even closer than she thought he was. "It's really something to see the fae work their magic. I hope this works and saves all your lives." He peered down at her, and she tried to take the last words he spoke in stride.

"You made a promise to my father, King Cullen," she muttered to herself.

"Aye, that I did. But I am not who you need to worry about."

"Point taken. Now please give me room to do this."

Cullen leaned in and whispered, "I am sure this will work."

Rage boiled up from within her. "It would. If you took a step back, I could truly begin." She huffed instinctively, raising her arms and shoving him away.

Hew, Brogan, and Dylan all took an instinctive step back. It was obvious Aoife's actions shocked them. The three men tensed, waiting for their king's reaction.

But Cullen seemed unruffled as he caught Aoife's arm and issued a mild warning before walking away. "I'll leave you to do your work then, but I wouldn't do *that* again."

She scowled and fought the urge to punch him in the nose. "You're the one invading my space. Maybe you shouldn't interrupt when I'm healing."

Brogan nervously licked his lips, leaning close to Dylan. "She's got spirit. I'll give her that," he murmured. Dylan shook his head in amazement.

Aoife didn't understand the big fuss, but then she realized Hew and Brogan were not aware she was the fae princess, so her actions seemed incredibly brave or downright foolish. Maybe it was both. She didn't care.

When their whispers died down, she called forth her light again and sent waves of it through the children. Their bodies lit up the darkened room and all the men gasped behind her.

Aoife paid little mind to them and focused on the children, checking their foreheads again. Their fevers were gone, and the warmth of their cheeks steadily returned. She watched their chests next for even breathing. Up and down, they went in a rhythmic manner. Satisfied, she got up and faced her audience.

"Are you finished, or do you need more time?" Cullen asked while he propped his arm against the doorway and glared at her.

"No. I am done. They should be awake by tomorrow morning." She shot daggers with her eyes in his direction before softening her reaction as she turned to the woodsman, wonder etched across his features.

"Hmm. Good, good. Let's head back to the castle tonight then." Cullen said.

"Aye, my king, if we leave now, we'll get to the side entrance an hour after sunset." Dylan stood next to her, ready to escort her into that uncomfortable wagon they came in.

She glanced back at the two children one last time and headed out of the room. Brogan came up to her and whispered. "Their names are Elsie and Ewan. I wanted you to know."

"Thank you for telling me. I know this isn't easy. Be with them now until they wake. They need you there. Talk to them, call them back to you, call them back home and hold both their hands while you say this. Oh, and take them outside to get sunlight and fresh air."

She sent one last spark of her healing light to him as he brushed by her. With a little extra energy, she knew they could power through.

Dylan led her outside and back into her seat. The sun was making its descent when the wheels creaked to life and rolled them forward on their way to the castle. She only heard tales about.

As they traveled further, their progress became swifter and the ride more punishing over the uneven earth. When he spoke, he mentioned random facts about Nairn and the road they traveled on. Some of what he said sounded interesting, and she peered out the left window to see massive fields of grain and other vegetation. All cultivated by farmers, according to him. They differed from what Erainn did, and she wanted to learn more.

"Aye, that's the druid's territory. Not mine. I am sure he can share more details with you when ya settle in more," he said.

"Sounds wonderful," she mumbled under her breath, before she turned to look up at him, offering a smile.

When they were closer to their destination, he handed her a small candy from his satchel. Efi gladly accepted and thanked him. The sweetness of honey tantalized her tongue while she watched the last bits of light fade behind the tree line. The orange and violet sky languidly transformed into dark blue as night took over the day.

Excitement and wonder filled her to the brim. Despite the circumstances, she had always wanted to see the human castle nestled in the Bothain mountains with the city of Falkirth surrounding it. Tales of its splendor had filled her youth and soon she'd see it for herself.

She peeped her head out once more and saw the famed stone bridge that led into the city. They had constructed the entire city wall encircling the mountain's edge. Instead of taking the bridge, they traveled down a small hill and under it. The path they took led them to the side of the castle. Dylan ushered her out into the night once the wagon came to a full stop.

The king and his guards surrounded her and guided her up a large flight of stairs that seemed to twist and turn forever. She couldn't see anything in front of her besides steel armor and cloaks, with swords dangling from their sides. They soon entered through a gate that led straight into the castle grounds.

Like the tales she heard, the castle was carved into the mountainside. The stairs, the walls, every bit was a hollowed-out piece of the earth. There was a large waterfall centered between two enormous doors that greeted her first. The water flowed down through the floor and traveled into the city below.

She shuddered with thoughts of sleeping in her new prison. She was used to lush gardens, not cold uncaring walls, and an even colder people from what she'd be told.

The guards opened a door as tall as oaks into a massive hall. A grand feast was being served to a large crowd. The smell of cooked flesh made her gag.

The king talked with several men before proceeding ahead. They all went quiet and stared at her. Suspicion in their eyes. She turned away and saw him. The devious man from her trial. His crooked smile made her seethe with hatred for him. *Nathair, just the sight of him makes my skin crawl.* There was something deeply wrong with him. A crushing feeling pulsed around his person and made her wish she was far across the room instead.

He stood up and walked in her direction. His fists were balled up, but his face remained blank. He had almost made it to her side when Dylan stepped in front of her and blocked him from coming any closer.

"Hey there Nat. Come to harass King Cullen's ward again?"

"Pfft. Of course not. I wanted to see how our lady fared the trip."

"She did fine."

"And the children?"

"Alive and well. But you should learn to mind your business."

"The king's affairs are my business."

"Oh please, you gutter rat. Cullen sees straight through your act. You poke your nose around where you're unwanted all the time- off with ya."

"I'd hold yer tongue if you know what's good, Dylan." Nat backed away slowly and turned to sit back down.

Dylan scoffed at him. "Say it to my face now. Ya runt of a man."

Dylan directed her to more stairs. "Off to the living quarters and away from this drab," He lowered his voice and pulled her closer to him. "If he tries to get you alone, please tell me and I'll see to him right away. We only keep him around because old king Whelan swears he's a trusted council member. I think he's a wolf parading around in sheep's skin. A dirty snake hidden in the brush, ready to strike when you are not looking."

She stood there in shock. He had remained quiet for the entirety of both their trips. Had barely spoken to her and now he was telling her all this.

"Well, follow me pri-lady Aoife." Dylan's eyes shifted to where Nat sat. His back turned and attention elsewhere.

More guards came and helped escort her further to the stairs. Once they reached the second set, it was only Dylan and her. *Do these damned stairs ever end? What a horrible place to live.*

"Are those people in the huge hall part of the court? That's quite a lot of humans. Err, I mean people," she asked.

Dylan laughed, "Nae, it's the old king's formal farewell despite King Cullen being in charge for years. Been going on a damned week now. I'll be glad when it's over."

"Oh, I see. Will I meet him soon?"

"I suppose so. He's very ill. You're a healer, though. Hmm. I wonder if the king intends to ask for your help." He turned left down a long hallway and motioned for her to follow.

"Your quarters are next to the King's."

"Can I ask you why everyone calls him the Wolf King?"

"Aye, it's a myth that says all the kings of Nairn share lineage with the Ostraige Werewolves. Nothing but silly folktales. The wolf is also the royal coat of arms, though. So, I suppose it's a bit of both."

"I see."

"Here's yer room, miss." Dylan opened a door and led her in.

Dark blue tapestries with wolves in various scenes draped the walls. For a myth, there sure was a lot of wolf art and other things carved into the very walls with magical knots wrapped around them.

She inspected her new room. A large bed with a thick blanket and large stuffed pillows sat centered in the room. A desk was near an open window. One side led out to a balcony, and she noticed a private bathing area on her left.

"You're to stay here until we hear from Brogan."

"I can't go anywhere else?"

"Not until the king tells me otherwise. G'night lass."

She closed her eyes and took a deep breath. It would take all of her to survive being trapped inside.

She inspected the room some more, looking for anything that might point her to a change of fresh clothes.

Around the bed, tucked near a sizable wardrobe, lay Orla's chest. *How did it get here?* She wondered for a second, but this was her godsmother—she always had a trick up her sleeve and more magic than anyone cared to admit. Though her father wore the crown, Orla's power ran far deeper. Ancient magic flowed strongly through the old crone's veins; her abilities shrouded in mystery. Orla only permitted Aoife brief glimpses past those veils, unraveling her secrets slowly in her own time. When and what she shared was hers to decide, no matter Aoife's pleas otherwise.

Even the connection Orla had with her mother was unknown to her, besides being named her godsparent if something ever happened—which it did. Aoife had spent years mourning her mother's death. Yet she was grateful for the bond her godsmother and her had built and shared over the years. Orla had been mother when her own wasn't there.

Aoife shook the thoughts of her mother and Orla away and cracked open the chest: she found several of her own dresses, a light nightgown, and her favorite pair of shoes. She whispered *a thank you* before closing it and taking out her nightwear.

A slight nip filled the air as her fingers rubbed the thin fabric in her hands. *Maybe there is something warmer available.* She searched the wardrobe and found a soft but thick pastel blue nightgown. Efi slipped off her pink dress and slid right into the night clothes and breathed deeply. *I am ready for this day to end*. She threw back the blankets on the bed and sat on the edge of the mattress. Exhaustion set in once she curled up into it, the softness of the bedding lulling her to sleep.

Her eyes grew heavy, but then she heard Dylan and the king talk outside her door. She only caught pieces of their conversion. More guards, monitor you know who. *I know who they're talking about.* She heard the door creak open but kept her eyes closed, pretending she was asleep. Aoife didn't want more company or talking until morning. She sensed someone standing near for several moments before the rustling of a cloak sounded in her ears.

She creaked one eye slightly open and saw Cullen extinguish the wall lanterns before departing. As soon as the door shut, weariness flooded through her. She surrendered to its pull, eyelids sinking closed. Within moments, she drifted into an exhausted, dreamless sleep.

SEVEN

CULLEN

The Promise

After being away all day, Cullen wasted no time in visiting his father once they settled Aoife into her chamber. He delved out orders to the guard, then entered his da's room to inform him of the trial's outcome and the decision reached.

Da was distraught about allowing a fae woman to stay in the castle—no doubt the result of Nat's poisonous whisperings in his ear while he was away.

"I don't know why you trust that man," Cullen mumbled before his father shuffled off to his privy chamber, leaving him standing alone. But a moment later, his father wandered back in, face clouded in confusion.

"What were we just talking about, son?" he asked weakly before returning to his favorite books, mind already gone.

The illness blinded him to Nat's manipulations. While Cullen wished he could ban Nat from seeing his father completely, he knew the repercussions if he refused his father at all. Not when the consequences of his temper were so unpredictable. He said nothing and hugged his father's frail and aging body gently.

It pained Cullen to see the once-mighty king reduced to this. And the Gods hadn't seen fit to take him yet, so Cullen kept him as comfortable as he could, but he also had to keep his father locked up. The human body appeared weak, but the wolf could still hurt those around him.

Cullen retreated to his own chambers, pouring a pint of ale, hoping to clear his head. A rap at the door scattered his thoughts.

"Aye, is that you Dylan? Come on in," he said before taking a swig of ale.

"Dylan and Riordan, sire."

His two most trusted advisers sauntered in. He beckoned them to sit down.

Dylan scanned the room once over before he spoke, "Nat's is up to something, my king."

"No need to address me so formally. It's just the three of us."

"I agree with Dylan. He'll make a play for the throne." Riordan sat down in a chair across from him.

"Keep our allies close and enemies closer." Cullen murmured, fingers idly stroking through his beard as he contemplated those words. He took a long draught of ale before setting the mug down with a thud.

Dylan lowered his voice. "What about the princess?"

Cullen's thumb and forefinger tugged at a wiry golden strand of his beard, eyebrows drawing together pensively. Having the fae princess under his roof was a precarious gamble, he knew, but the fae's healing power and knowledge of the land surpassed their own. They needed her here now, to fight whatever curse was spreading.

He couldn't tell his counsel just yet, but Torin had mentioned the Shadow Court. Things were far worse than he originally thought, and they needed their alliance alive and well.

"Keep that a secret and keep her safe. We can't afford to lose Erainn as an ally. The rangers in Kirkwall reported constant faint light pulsing around the Twisted Tree that leads into Faery. The fair folk are crossing through the portal more once more. Problem is, none of our men have caught wind of their whereabouts. This troubles me."

"So, we prepare for what could be at our doorstep,

along with what's already living within our own borders." Riordan let out a hard sigh.

"Aye. Keep a watchful eye on Aoife until we know what old Nat's up to. Riordan, please see she has what she needs until I can visit her. It could be the next few days before that happens. All depends on the next reports as more roll in."

"It will be done."

"Dylan, you're on personal guard duty."

"She's safe with me, but Cullen, what about you?" Dylan didn't look happy with him, but he trusted no one else as much as them.

"There is nobody else I trust. The two of you are my truest confidants, understood?" his focus shifted back and forth between Dylan and Riordan. They nodded, but Dylan's eyes betrayed his lingering concern. "I'll be fine, or have you forgotten what we are?" Cullen reassured him with a wry smile.

"No, sire." Dylan said.

Riordan's brow furrowed; his expression deeply troubled. He opened his mouth to speak, then seemed to think better of it and closed it again, a muscle in his jaw ticking.

"Riordan, I promise I won't tear Nat up in wolf form. Well, maybe a little. If he attacks with all his forces, I make no promises. I'll do what I have to, to protect myself and our kingdom, and the alliance we have with Erainn."

"But the people..."

"I'm sick of hiding. The people whisper about it all the time." Cullen brushed off his friend's concerns. He was the Wolf King. Kind but brutal. Feared by some and loved by many. The people would rally with him. He had always taken care of them when their lords had not.

Riordan puffed off a breath of frustration. "Consider the repercussions, my king. Rumored stories and the truth are two different beasts."

"I have. Now leave me." Cullen clapped them both on the back before getting up and walking out to check on his ward. He opened the door and found her in bed, fast asleep.

The first time he saw her, his emotions were mixed. She was beautiful, full of passion, but too quick to action. She needed to temper her response and make better decisions. He stood there a moment, letting the connection they shared pulse through him. *What does it mean? Is she?* He dimmed the lanterns and crept back to the door. Cullen glanced over his shoulder—he wasn't too sure he believed her side of the story. She claimed innocence, but he saw darkness in her. Not even she was aware of it. Which puzzled him further.

He had tried to mention what he sensed to his friend, but Torin rejected the idea. He claimed it was the lingering effects of the poison. Maybe he was right. Only time would tell if she was truly friend or foe.

Dark times lay ahead for them all. A shift in the wind pricked at his skin and attacked all his senses. He couldn't be sure of anything. Even his own feelings.

Time would provide the answers. He hoped there was enough of it. After removing his armor, he stood on the balcony and jumped down to the roof in a flash. Once his feet landed on the grass below, he took off, running into the darkened forest.

EIGHT

AOIFE

And Time Passes

THE MOURNFUL HOWLS OF WOLVES PIERCED THE STILL morning air, startling Aoife awake. Heart pounding, she realized they were close to castle grounds. Wolves avoided crossing into Erainn, and their eerie howls were a distant sound she rarely heard. The chilling volume of their cries was unfamiliar, setting her nerves on edge.

Pale streams of daylight poured in from a small upper window. Shivering, Aoife crossed the icy stone floor on bare feet to peer outside. The world beyond was dappled in breaks of leaking light. The forest remained swallowed in inky shadows, with no sign of the creatures that had shattered the tranquility of her sleep.

Grabbing a thick woolen shawl, she wrapped it tight around her shoulders to fight off the penetrating cold emitting from the ancient stone walls. Aoife already missed home. The chill of the mountains sank to the bone, unlike the cool weather in the valleys of her kingdom. *I wonder how long it will take me to adjust to this change.* She ran a hand over the smooth contours of the wall, longing to feel the vibrant magic she often sensed when conversing with the trees, but this felt empty.

She wandered around her room, getting a better look at it as more light filled her chamber. Across from the fireplace was an ivory wooden door—with a beautiful white she-wolf and her pups carved in the center. Aoife pushed the door open and gasped.

The washroom area was spectacular and unusual. A natural hot spring ran through the wall and floor, disappearing into the depths of what she assumed was the mountain itself. An ornate oval tub carved from granite sat in the middle of the room, steaming hot. She couldn't wait to test it out, but she wanted to explore the other areas first.

There was another wash area with a stone seat recessed into the wall. Many kinds of soap were on a shelf next to it, and it looked like the crafters of the keep had chiseled a deep hole in the floor. There was a smaller waterfall pouring into the hot spring with a pull string connected to it. Curiosity overcame her, and she pulled on it. The water redirected into the long pipe and out a small bucket with many holes and rained down right in front of her. Startled, she stepped back, releasing the string, and the water stopped.

This was something she hadn't seen before; Orla had told her about different human inventions, but never this one. She was used to the hot pools beneath the palace and the large baths where the unicorns would purify the water as needed. She'd have to ask how everything worked in here when she could. Including the permanent chamber pot tucked in the corner. A soft rap at the door drew her attention. Before she could respond, it creaked open.

"Are you suitable for company, my lady?" an unfamiliar voice rumbled.

"Yes," Aoife called, stepping out from the washroom.

A man with a wild, golden mane entered. His eyes widened at the sight of her in her nightclothes. Spinning abruptly, he faced the closed door.

"I thought you said you were dressed," he remarked gruffly.

Aoife frowned, confused. “I am dressed, clothed. What have you?”

“Do the fae often receive guests in their bedclothes?” he asked, keeping his back turned.

Comprehension dawned on her. “Well, no sir, but clothing is all the same, so if someone comes calling early, we don’t fuss over changing. Did I offend you?”

“Nae, my lady, but here in Nairn, one often dresses for the day before accepting visitors.”

“Oh! Oh my! Of course.” She flushed, rushing over to Orla’s chest and discovered a new dress. It was the green one she had worn the other day, the one she called her favorite *thank you ma*. Aoife stepped into the private dressing area with her clothes. “Please give me a moment and I will be right with you.”

“I’ll take my leave outside a minute then,” the man said before he took a step out the door.

Aoife wiggled out of the nightgown and got her clothes on. Checking herself in the mirror, she fixed her hair into a thick bun on top of her head, loose strand fell in front of her face, and she twirled them a bit with her fingers and made her way to the door.

“My apologies. I am ready now.”

The man reentered the room and closed the door behind him. “We haven’t met yet. I am Riordan,” he said, bowing and taking her hand in his, he grazed a light kiss over her knuckles. "A pleasure to make your acquaintance at last."

"You're the Druid," she said matter of fact.

"Indeed, I am. How'd you know?"

"I sensed your power when you came in the first time."

His eyebrow crooked up, and his eyes studied hers. "I was unaware that fae folk could sense human magic."

She smiled vaguely. "Not all fae can," she said.

"I see. Well, let's begin the day. Servants will serve breakfast here in your room. Dinner will be with the king in his private quarters when he calls on you. Lunch will vary depending on what we do that day. I'll show you around Falkirth too, but for now, you are to stay close to castle grounds."

"Do you have an area with gardens, trees, and flowers? And can you explain how everything works in this room to me? Especially the washroom."

"Yes, we will have tea there this afternoon. And, of course, I can show you before we head out. It's simple. You pull the string down and attach the large bead here, stand underneath there, wash your body, rinse, then soak in the hot spring if you wish. We don't dirty up the water if we can help it."

"Oh, that is interesting. Tell me more about how humans keep things clean and everything else. I'm extremely curious since the fae do things differently."

"It would be my honor to teach you. I would love to hear what the fae do too. On another note, is there anything you need that I can get for you to make your stay more comfortable?" he asked.

"As much time outside as possible," she replied.

"In time, my lady, but for now." He edged in closer to her and whispered, "You need to stay close to me and Dylan, just in case. You're not safe here. I will prolong our time in the garden if it pleases you."

"It would. I appreciate your willingness to accommodate."

She took deep breaths after that and tried to contain her feelings. Aoife had never stayed inside the palace in Erainn for very long and made a habit of staying out on her missions for as long as possible to avoid those walls that felt like they were crushing in on her, and now she would have to deal with living in Nairn's fortress. She'd miss her home. At least there they had light marbled walls. The ones here were dark gray and gloomy.

"I can see that you are taking the situation in stride. Once things settle down and the people see the fae helping, things will change. Right now, most of the court knows the fae in Erainn are friends, not enemies, but the curse and dark fae being spotted have many of our people on edge. I promise to bring everything that you require and will ensure your stay is comfortable," Riordan said.

"Well then, let's get to it. What do I need to do to show everyone here I mean no harm?" she asked.

"Do you know anything about this curse or the magics that created it? What can we do to stop it from spreading?" he said.

"You'll need fire, and to clear out the area of all infected florae. It's not dark fae magic, it's the work of a daemon. My father said they are a type of Faelyn though, but I am not sure what that means. We need to send someone to Erainn and ask if the fire is working and what type of protective measures they are putting in place."

He sat down in the other chair across from her and sat hunched over his knees, his gaze solely on her.

"Interesting. Can you tell me more about this daemon? And what made you decide fire would stop it?"

"Of course. Anything to help. This affects both our lands."

Over the next hour, they discussed what they knew of the curse. Riordan also explained the workings of her chamber and promised to show her the gardens after. Though sympathetic to her need for more freedom, he urged Aoife to remain close for now. In turn, she shared what she could about fae magic and healing the blighted land. Despite the circumstances, she took an immediate liking to the druid and was glad to have his company for the coming months.

Riordan promised a full tour of the castle and its grounds next. When they opened the door to head out, Dylan was waiting. He immediately fell in line behind them and escorted them everywhere; always keeping a watchful eye on her.

As they walked through the courtyard, a line of subjects trailed out beyond the doors. Hush gasps and whispered lingered in the air when they passed by. Aoife smiled curtly and lowered her head. She wanted to earn the respect of these people to show them she meant no harm.

Glimpsing Cullen upon his throne, she sensed the stress building within him. He stole a quick glance her way and the same spark she felt upon meeting him coursed through her veins. His gaze locked on hers, and his face was telling. He sensed it, too. *What does this mean, Wolf King?*

Before another thought crossed her mind, Nathair

strolled in like he owned the place. His arrogance oozing off his robes. He immediately addressed the king, and Cullen's expression changed to disdain. "Good king Cullen I would have a word with you."

"Sir Nathair Mac an Ghirr, I will have that word as soon as I finish speaking to the others behind you." Cullen said. A smirk crossed his face as Nathair turned red with anger.

"Serves him right for thinking he is above everyone else who's been waiting." Dylan whispered.

Aoife let him know she agreed. Before Nat saw them in the hall, they took off in the direction they came and back into the gardens.

"Dare I say that was close? I have orders to keep *that* man as far away from you as possible." Dylan huffed.

"There's something sinister brewing within him. I thank you for getting us out of there," Aoife said.

"Well, to tea and more conversations on magic? To pass the time until dinner with the king." Riordan asked.

"I'd love that."

The evening came and her nerves twisted around her like bindweed, threatening to choke her composure. Riordan had left her in Cullen's private quarters to await his arrival. Curiosity overpowered her while she waited. Against her better judgment, she investigated the area surrounding her. Leather maps with thick tombs lay on an oaken table in one corner of the room. Two swinging doors led to a bed chamber across from where she stood.

She knew snooping was unwise, but the urge to unravel the mysteries of this man, the Wolf King, compelled her onward. Letting her gaze wander, she was drawn to a tattered, worn book resting on a small table beside a stuffed armchair near the fireplace.

Its edges frayed and the covers slightly ajar. Unable to resist, she opened it carefully. Tucked inside, she discovered a delicate gold locket and pried it open, revealing a painted portrait within—a lovely blonde woman cradling a fair-haired babe on her lap: both mother and child were adorned in flowing ivory garb. The woman possessed a careworn yet gentle beauty, with long golden waves framing her porcelain face. It flowed down around her neck, flowing around her arms and child like a blanket of protection.

Sitting there on the lady's neck hung the same locket that Aoife held tenderly in her hands. She marveled at the intricate brushstrokes capturing their likenesses so vividly in paint. It had to be the king and his mother.

Footsteps sounded outside, and she snapped the locket shut in a panic as Cullen strode in. His eyes narrowed, seeing it in her hand.

"That does not belong to you," he said sharply, snatching it away. He placed it gently between the book and closed it. His stare bared down on her. The intensity of his scrutiny made her flush.

"I'm sorry. I've been waiting for what seems like an hour. Was she your mother? She was lovely." Aoife spoke meekly.

Cullen's jaw clenched; reluctance written across his face. Finally, he nodded.

"She died when I was young, and that is all you need to know. I'll speak no more on the matter."

"I'm sorry to bring up old wounds. Forgive me." she paused. "I want to know who you are. I–" Her voice was barely audible.

He interrupted. "Leave it be. Dinner will arrive soon. Let us sit at the table." He pointed to the large dining area in a separate room with an open archway. She rushed to his side, and he ushered her into a seat.

"My mother died when I was young too," she whispered, sitting in the chair he pulled out for her.

Cullen gave a curt nod and changed the subject.

"Have you and Riordan gleaned any information on combating this curse?"

"Yes, we spoke at length about what I think needs to be done, but we should send a message to my father and ask if sending the drakes helped. I suggested fire to stop the spread. And cleaning out the infected areas the best we can."

"I will see that it is done. On both accounts. Now, how do you like your quarters?" he asked.

She stiffened up, not knowing what to say next. Did she speak the truth? Everything here was foreign and harsh compared to life in Erainn. The magic they held had changed the land there. The mountains had a certain chill she couldn't shake off.

"Well?" his eyebrow ticked up.

"It's lovely. Thank you for your hospitality."

"Stark change from the woman who threw her fists my way yesterday." He chuckled.

"If I may be so bold, you interrupted me. Any man worth his salt should know to keep quiet when a woman is working."

He guffawed and slapped his thigh. "Very bold indeed." He relaxed in his seat and three servants came in with several large platters of food.

"I wasn't sure what the fae ate, so I asked for an assortment of meats, vegetables, and fruit. Take what you like. There is also a tray of baked goods." He grabbed a large dinner roll and took an enormous bite before piling potatoes and roast beef in heaping mounds on his plate.

"We eat less meat, if any at all. I will eat eggs and honey."

"Aye! Tell Iona the needs of our guest when you return to the kitchens Roy."

"Yes, your highness." Roy said, before shuffling out of the room.

"Well, let's eat."

And she did, savoring each roasted vegetable and delicious pieces of fruit she had never tasted before. The bread was absolutely divine and as good as Orla's, but she'd never tell her that.

Cullen kept their conversation to a minimum. She shouldn't have let her curiosity get the better of her. She needed to understand the man she was working with. *If I am to be an emissary for Erainn, he needs to get to know me so we can work together.* She wished he was easier to converse with and had a feeling thing would not be as equable as they had been with Riordan. *At least he wants to talk with me and treats me as an equal. I hope the king in front of me can do the same someday.*

She recalled what her father said about him. But did the Wolf King need to be coarse with every action he took? Wasn't there room for more? Only time would tell if there was more to his rough exterior.

NINE

AOIFE

Trouble is, as Trouble Does

Two weeks later, Efi found herself in trouble after dinner when she had roamed the halls alone. She stumbled upon the library and hid from Dylan so she could explore it alone. The stonemasons who built the castle had carved all the bookshelves that lined the walls into the rock itself. This had to be the innermost part of the mountain as some shelves had natural gems clusters protruding out from them.

Long ladders on small wheels sat atop a metal bar. Thick leather-bound books filled each case to the brim. A bundle of scrolls sat stacked on a table with a polished stone top. She constantly found herself amazed and appalled by the work of those ancient builders that brought Nairn to life. She was untying the string around one when she heard the king's voice behind her.

"Aoife? What are you doing here alone?" Cullen asked.

She whirled around to find him standing directly behind her.

She lied, "I am waiting here for Dylan. I said I'd keep myself hidden. Tucked away in a corner from prying eyes."

"I see. We seem to have a moment then. I am waiting for Grannd to contact me about the children. He is the lord in charge of the villages closest to the border where the incident occurred. From what I heard, there is progress each day. I will have a formal report soon. He should arrive any day." He said.

"Thank you for letting me know. I was worried," she replied.

"Is everything to your liking? The room? Your schedule?" inquired Cullen.

Aoife's shoulders fell. "I could use more time outside, but Riordan said that would come later."

"Aye, it will. Things unfolded differently from what I imagined. I am sorry for my absence. Some lords are not happy with my choice to have you here in Nairn. I've been busy debating them the last few days." Cullen said.

A guard approached them and cleared his throat.

"Sire, you're needed in the great hall." He stood erect and saluted his king.

"Again," Cullen sighed.

"I will see you soon, I hope. I'd like to get to know you better," she whispered.

"Soon. Best be ready for when Dylan finds you." He winked before promptly heading out.

Her mouth dropped open. He knew she had fibbed. She went back to flipping through the books on a table nearby. An hour passed before the guards found her and Dylan came barreling in, only to chase her back to her room after. He even threatened to lock the door this time.

All she could do was apologize profusely and beg him for a second chance. She promised she'd stay in her room. He left her to her own devices, but shut the door hard.

Dylan had told her he would return to escort her to dinner, but she grew sick of the wait and opened the door to room her softly and snuck out. *I feel like a caged bird. Struggling to get out.* Dylan's back faced her, so she made a mad dash to the hallway across from her. She turned a corner and there was another door ajar.

At first, she whirled around to return and face Dylan's ire, but curiosity got the better of her and she pushed it open. A frail-looking man sat up in his bed. He had similar features to Cullen, except his hair was solid gray.

"Who are you, miss?" he asked.

Efi froze in her tracks. "I am Aoife," she said.

"Oh, the fae woman my son mentioned."

She crept closer to get a better look at him. "Are you king Whelan?" she asked.

"King no more. My son is. I'm so proud of him. I wish he was here. He said he would come with you, but where is he?"

"Oh no, I snuck out of my room. I feel smothered by the walls and wish I could be in fields of green or in the trees." She admitted.

The old king chuckled at her answer. "It will be our secret. My mind feels clear for the moment. Come closer, would you?"

She stepped up to the edge of the bed and stood by his right side. He asked her more questions, and she tried her best to answer. He asked about her father and why she was here. "I miss my friend Torin. He's a good man. Best of the fair folk I know."

Efi fell silent and stared down at the floor.

"You are not too sure? Of your own father?" he asked.

Aoife sighed. "He forced me to come here, and it feels like he sent me to my death."

"No, he'd never do that. Don't fret, you will survive this. My son would never let that happen."

"I hope so." She said.

"Have faith, child. Can I ask one more question of you?" He held her hand in his.

"Yes, of course." She patted his arm and smiled down at him.

"You can help me. I am sick, but the sickness is not natural. Can you figure what it is?"

"What do you mean?" Aoife arched back, knowing good and well what he was asking of her.

"There is something unnatural causing it. I lose myself. Like right now, I have no idea how I ended up in this bed."

"I'm sorry to hear this. I'd like to help, but are you sure? You know what you are asking of me, correct?" she reached out to hold one of his hands in both of hers.

"I am. Do what you must. I am ready. This thing, whatever it may be... feels like I'm cursed to suffer for eternity. The God's keep me here. For what reason I never understand." He closed his eyes and held in a deep breath.

When she touched him with full magic in tow, she felt a darkness wash over them both. His body shook all over. She swiftly pulled away and calmed him.

"What was that?" His face washed with fear.

Her hands trembled. "I don't know. I've never come across anything like this."

"Let's try again." He stuck out his hand for her to grab.

"I don't think that's a good idea." Aoife took a step back.

"Please, I see visions of Cullen, the sadness, the weight of the kingdom he bears—it's killing me," he begged her.

"But–"

"Please, and this time, don't let go. You hear me? I have a feeling I'll be all right. I am safe in your hands. Your healing feels very much like your father's." He cracked a smile, with an outstretched hand waiting to be grasped.

"Are you sure? You barely know me."

"Ah yes, but if you're anything like your father. My trust is not misplaced. Please, before Nat visits."

"Nat? I thought he was your..."

"No, this has something to do with him, but I cannot speak the words to Cullen. The opposite rolls off my lips or I can't speak at all." His eyes flared with anger.

"A curse, not a natural illness?" She raised her eyebrow.

"Maybe?" he shrugged.

"I don't like that snake of a man one bit. I'll do it and will use my healer's light on you, too."

"You have the healer's light like your father? Do you have any gifts from your mother, too?"

"I do. You knew my mother?"

"I did. Maeve was a wonderful friend."

"I'm sorry. My memories of her have faded. I was never told much about you, either."

"Seems Torin has kept much from his children. I might have to have a word with him if I make it out of this."

"You will. I promise. Are you ready?"

"Ready." He placed his hands into hers.

The room darkened again, and the world spun the moment they touched. Efi held on tight. The old king's body convulsed. She struggled to find the source of what caused his sickness as fast as she could. She searched his body with her mind. His entire system was contaminated, resembling the poison within the trees. *How could this be? Are they linked? But how? The other creatures were dead, and he lives?*

She tried to release his hand, but his grip tightened. A strength she hadn't expected crushed her fingers, and she struggled to pull herself free. Every single piece of his pain leached into her system, and they both screamed out in agony. She tugged away at their interconnected hands once more, but the connection remained. Flashes of a fanged mouth and a devilish grin engulfed her vision.

"I can't break loose! Whatever this is, it won't release me," she yelped.

King Whelan thrashed about harder. He whipped her arm around while she tried again to get loose.

She forced her healer's light through that hand and into him. As she did this, Cullen and the guards came barging in on the scene.

"I'm struggling to let go. I need help! Pull my hand out of his!" she screamed.

"What the hell is going on?" He belted out. Cullen grabbed her arm and pulled. But it didn't work. Soon he had her by the waist, forcing all his weight backward, his feet gliding across the floor.

Aoife cried out, "Release me!" Suddenly the connection broke and old King Whelan yowled, then passed out. Her body flew backward into Cullen and they fell to the ground.

"What did you do?" he gasped.

"Searching for answers. The poison. It's in..." She scrambled off him. She pivoted to grip her hands on the floor beneath her. His face inches away from hers. She apologized, but then slipped and landed on top of him.

"Oh, my gods! Are you okay?" her cheeks flushed.

He mumbled beneath her and grabbed her waist, then sat her down beside him and sprung up. "I'm fine. Now explain yourself. Why are you in here and what were you doing to my father?"

His hand brushed hers as he got up, and sparks shot through her, overloading her senses. Cullen shivered, then rushed to check on his father and called out for Riordan. When he came running in, his face turned sheet white when he saw Aoife in the room.

"What happened, my king? Everyone out, besides the two of you." He pointed to her and Cullen.

"Aoife, you need to tell me what you did. Every detail right now," Riordan said.

"He asked me to find the source of his sickness. I wanted to assist him. I grabbed his hand and then this happened. He immediately started shaking all over, but he told me to continue. I said no, and he pleaded with me. I, I am so sorry... only wanted to help, and he begged me. He said Nathair had a–"

"Enough! I don't want to hear anymore. Just fix him." Cullen whipped around and stomped toward her.

She shrunk down as he towered over her. He relaxed when he saw the frightened look on her face. His face slacked, and he shook his head and jolted back. His body shook. She tried to reach out, but brought her hand back to her chest. She rested her chin on it and kept her eyes on the ground.

"King Cullen, I said I am sorry. I heal. It's what I do. I cannot stand by and watch someone suffer as he does. Please... forgive me. I meant no harm."

"Cullen, calm down. Your father, He's alright and he will be fine." Riordan slipped between them.

His hand touched the king's shoulder, and he relaxed. As soon as the Wolf King sat back down, the druid went and checked King Whelan again. She headed to the door and stood in the hallway.

"I told you to keep a close eye on her. What the hell? I don't mind that she checked, but alone. Oh Gods. Are you sure he's all right?"

Riordan breathed, "Cullen, she didn't hurt him. Look he's waking."

"Cullen, my boy, is that you? Where's Torin? Where's Maeve? She, the young woman, was such a lovely light." Whelan tried to sit up, but weakness overtook him.

"Take her to room, now."

"King Cullen please," Aoife took a few steps in his direction.

His shoulders shook. "Get out of here. Not right now, please. I need a few moments, both of you *out*."

"But I have something I need to tell you," she said.

Riordan gently took hold of her arm and walked her out.

"Aoife, what were you thinking?" he asked her on the way back to her chamber.

"Old king Whelan is not sick. *He's cursed.* Someone did this to him. It's the same poison in the trees. Riordan, I have to tell him. This can't wait. This is serious. I am not sure how he's even alive. He should be dead."

Riordan stopped in his tracks. "Speak no more of this until I come to see you later, understand?" He looked her dead in the eye.

"Understood."

He ushered into her room and shut the door behind him.

I've really done it now. The king surely wants me dead or gone after this. I almost killed his father. I need to think first before leaping into action. She sat on the floor near the window and crawled under the desk. It*'s not the Elder Tree, but it will do.* Then she sat there wishing she was visiting Nightwind and Dessa as she waited for the Wolf King to descend upon her.

TEN

CULLEN

Calm the Rage

CULLEN SAT IN A CHAIR NEXT TO HIS FATHER'S BED. *What had she been thinking? Was she out of her mind?* Torin had been right; she was much too brash as he had once been.

"Sire. She was trying to help." Riordan stepped into the room and braced himself against the wall by the old king's bed.

"At what cost? You weren't here. You didn't see his body; I thought him possessed!"

"She told me something very unsettling." Riordan checked Whelan again.

"What did she tell you?" Cullen asked.

"That the toxin from the forest is in your father's

veins. His sickness is a curse. She's not wrong. It makes sense now and I think it is Nat's doing."

"It seems *all* things lead back to that retched man. We need to take care of him once and for all."

"Not yet. We don't have proof. While I trust Aoife's thoughts on the matter. I don't think the King's Counsel will see it as truth. There are seeds of mistrust. Some don't believe Erainn to be our ally like you say. Nat fuels that fire too. We need something more solid before we confront him." Riordan said.

"I need you to focus on finding proof." Cullen turned to face his friend.

"Yes, my king. In the meantime, please be gentle with her. She means well."

"She's an adult. Stop acting like she's a child I must coddle. She made choices and must deal with the consequences. This was almost too far, especially after the incident involving the children. She's lucky it was my personal guard and me. What if it had been Nat? What then?"

"Ah, this is where you're only half right. *By all accounts,* she is a grown woman, but the fae live longer lives than we do. She is *just* coming into adulthood. Even then, they draw it out until they reach thirty. Be soft with her. The lives of fae differ greatly from our own. Again, she is on our side and we need to trust her."

"I'll try. He's all I left of my family. Surely you can't blame me for my reaction."

"I understand your pain, as my loss has been great as well. I'll take my leave and return to check on him later." Riordan bowed and began exiting the door.

Cullen fixed the blankets around his father. "I know you understand, my friend. More than most. I must see to my father now." His words trailed as he watched his second in command leave the room.

"Father, what were you thinking?"

Whelan cracked one eye open. His words clear and direct. "Is your wizard gone?"

"Da?" Cullen sat stunned.

Whelan opened both eyes and patted his son's arm. "I see that look my pup, wanted the druid gone, I did."

"Are you feeling any better?" Cullen asked.

"I only have a moment. Please don't be too harsh with the girl. Riordan is right. She wanted to lend a hand, and I asked her to, no I begged her. I am trapped and she tried to get me out. Oh Maeve, Torin, are you here? Your daughter. She did good you'd both be so proud and Freya. Is that you, my love? I missed you."

"What do you mean, trapped?" he leaned in closer to his da's face.

"Cullen, don't trust him and anyone who takes his

side. He's eyed our throne from the beginning. Kept him close I did. Keep an eye on him–the malef–Freya, our boy. You'd be proud. Where am I? What is this room?"

Cullen's shoulders fell, and he held his father's hand as he watched him lose clarity once more. Whelan dozed off to sleep, mumbling about his mother. He pulled the blankets up on him and headed to Aoife's room.

He knocked, then opened the door wide before entering. He searched around the chamber. At first, he didn't see her, but then he noticed her dress streaming out from under the desk across the room. And walked over to it.

"Lady Aoife." He crooked himself sideways and looked down under it.

"Why are you under there? You can come out. You have nothing to fear."

She looked up at him and then crawled out. She kept her head down and wouldn't look at him.

"I don't fault you for trying to help my da, but that was a very rash decision you made back there. What if something worse happened?"

"I'm sorry." Were the only words she eked out.

"I am sure you are. Next time, do as I have said. Keep to the areas you're allowed." He commanded.

"Stop treating me like I'm a child. I'm a woman. I

don't need someone constantly monitoring me. Stop acting like I'm your enemy, too. I'm not! You need to include me and let them see I am their ally." She suddenly spat out.

"Bold of you to speak like that after what's happened, or do I need to remind you of what you did in that forest? On my lands. What you did in that room just now?"

She gulped down whatever response she had planned and tried to walk away from him.

"You need to be more careful, Aoife. You're lucky most of those guards are loyal to me. The situation is far graver than before. You can't expect humans to trust anyone from Erainn when you're all fae."

"Most of them?" she glared up at him, "Which means not all of them. Things would improve if you'd stop keeping me cooped up. You think stone walls and conversations with your druid are enough? You're wrong. Let me meet some of the lords. Let me attend one of your council meetings so they can ask whatever they want of me."

Torin had warned him about his only daughter. She was something else. First, she was hiding under a damn table, but now she was taking chances by throwing his own words right back at him. He kind of liked her for it.

It was so easy for some of his subjects to agree,

just to please him. She didn't care about that in the least. *That darkness in her, though. It still unnerves a part of me. What does it mean? And how do I even bring it up?* He watched the fire within her burn hotter, and he smirked. Her face twisted up, but she held her tongue.

"I'll remind you again that you're considered an enemy until you prove otherwise. Hiding in the library, sneaking out of your room, and going into areas you don't belong in doesn't help your case. We need to proceed with caution. My people need to be eased into the idea of fae being here in our lands. Please trust that I'm getting us there."

"You need to trust me. I know myself and my mind to think I even questioned... never again. I wanted to help your father and I want to assist with the forest! This curse affects us all. I am well aware of what lies on the other side of the mountains. You think I'm childish and rash, but at least I don't sit on fighting for what is right. I understand the severity of the situation. They have drilled it into my head since the day I could understand. The Dark Fae want to destroy us and take Erainn and Nairn down because we stood up for ourselves and the humans helped us."

"I am not questioning your intent... more your actions like the ones you took with the shadow being and the children." He slid closer to her, and now they were inches apart.

"But I didn't hurt them. I swear."

"You said you were poisoned, and you found them like that after you attacked. You can't be sure of what happened. Your magic mixed with others is an unknown. How did they get hurt? We can't be certain of what you saw. Would you own it if you knew your fae powers had a hand in their injuries? Even if you didn't, at least admit the mistakes you made leading up to it."

"I hope you're as forthcoming about your own mistakes as you'd like me to be about mine. I can't change what happened. That creature was extremely powerful! If I have to stay here until I die to make recompense, I will! But stop punishing me by keeping me locked away. I'm tortured enough by the memory. Stop opening the wound and let it heal. Let's move on and do what's best for both our domains."

"Aoife, I'm not punishing you. There are things about this place... our human world you don't understand."

"Help me understand. Stop keeping me in the dark. I can't stand the emptiness of this castle or the grounds. The animals and trees are the things I miss most. I need to be surrounded by the forest... please!" she begged.

"The castle garden has trees and birds, probably some squirrels too. Oh, and those damned raccoons.

I'll even allow you to feed them if you want to. You'll be fine. You act like I've already given you a death sentence. I spared your life! Before we met at the border, my people wanted you dead, innocent or not." Exasperated, Cullen heaved a great sigh.

"Strike me down where I stand then and be done with this mess if I am such an inconvenience," she huffed, and shook the sword at his side.

"You're mad and acting like a spoiled brat. No wonder Torin conceded to this."

"What do you mean? This was your idea all along?" She lashed out at him, but he caught her flailing limbs and enveloped her in his embrace. Trapped against him, she thrashed wildly, trying to break free of his vice-like hold before finally stilling in defeat.

"Whoa, lassie, your father warned me about your temper."

"You don't understand fae at all if you think keeping me locked up in this soulless castle is best."

"The stone has a soul for those willing to calm themselves enough to feel it."

He could feel her rapid breathing and heart pounding in her chest. He exhaled a deep breath. Her dark green eyes and lush hair captivated him. She both infuriated and entranced him. He wasn't sure how to feel about all of this, especially her.

"Please, just once a week is all I ask. Outside of the walls. Take me yourself?" she whimpered as her body trembled in his grasp.

"I said I'd protect you, but what you did... What if someone else had been in there with him? Or if you were anywhere else without Dylan?"

Her breathing slowed, but she glared up at him with those defiantly beautiful eyes of hers. "I can defend myself," she huffed.

"That remains to be seen, but here in Nairn, the women let the men do most of the defending." He shifted his gaze down and enjoyed the rest of the view. Her eyes widened when she realized he wasn't looking directly at her face anymore, but she didn't move. Instead, she flicked her hair back and pressed her body into his, and kept her gaze right on him.

Not expecting her reaction, he paused, taking in her softness against his stomach, then let her go. She straightened her gown and scanned his face next. She took a step back from him and cocked her head.

"You said someone, but you meant Nat, didn't you?"

"Aye, but hold your tongue on the matter. Eyes and ears of the enemy are often closer than we think."

He eyed her closely again. She had ample breasts, sleek arms and small dainty hands. Her hips curved out from around her cinched waist. Her ears were petite, and he loved how they looked when just the tip peeked out from under her hair.

Everything about her body was perfect. The dress she wore hugged all the right places. He bit into his lip as he scanned her once more. He reached out to touch her wrist, but she pulled away and crossed her arms. She glared down at his hand. He thought for a second, she might slap it away.

"The way you're staring, I fear my hand might catch fire," he winked.

"Don't tempt me," Aoife grumbled, narrowing her eyes at him.

"I'll try not to," he replied with a roguish smirk. He enjoyed getting a rise out of her.

His upbeat expression quickly shifted, replaced with furrowed brows. "Join me for dinner tomorrow night. Please."

"Wow, did you... what?" she stammered in confusion.

"I changed the subject." He explained smoothly. "See you at sunset? I'll have the cooks make your favorite."

"What if I decline until you promise you'll take me out into the woods?" she asked, a mischievous glint in her eyes.

"Then you can go the rest of the night without food," he teased.

Her nostrils flared and her fist balled up. He had ruffed her feathers all right. Cullen tried to reach out to her, but she stormed off into the bathroom and closed the door. He rolled his eyes and said good night loud enough for all the castle to hear. She let out a frustrated scream as he left the room. He slammed the door good when he noticed Riordan was waiting out in the hallway for him.

"Well, that went well." Cullen straightened his stance.

"Sire, if that was your idea of it going well, no wonder you're unmarried still."

"Were you out here the whole time?"

"Yes. Not quite what I meant by go easy on the girl, Cullen. She feels guilty enough as it is about those kids."

"Watch yourself now. Riordan. You're still my subject."

ELEVEN

AOIFE

Dead Halls and Walls

SHE TOOK THREE LONG BREATHS. FIRST, SHE LANDED straight on top of him. How *embarrassing*. She also never had someone look at her like he did. She wasn't sure what to make of him.

He held her close to him, and that baffled her even more. Yet a part of her had liked every second of his skin touching hers. The other half wanted to reject the strange new feelings building within, but something deep inside stopped her. Her teeth dug into her lips as she thought about his body molding into hers. She wished he hadn't let go. Which only frustrated her more.

Aoife stood in the bathroom and waited for him to take his leave. Once she heard him slam the door, she undressed, soaped her body up, and rinsed before she got into the tub.

She carefully lowered herself into the steaming hot spring. *At least the water provides a small reprieve from this place.* She sank further into its depths and soaked for a good hour before heading off to bed.

Aoife woke before first day's light and got dressed right away. She had one goal in mind: to take part in the next council meeting, regardless of what Cullen wanted. After last night, she was sick of being told what to do, where to go, and how to act. Even with her mind telling her, it might be better to stop. If Cullen would include her more, he'd see that her only intention was to help.

She also needed to see how the council worked in a human court. Before Riordan came knocking on her door, she was out in the hall, walking to the chamber where all sessions were held. Dylan was trailing behind her, asking her what she had planned.

When the doors appeared, she ran to them. Dylan hollered for her to stop, but she creaked them open and slid in, sly as a fox. When she tried to shut the door Dylan's hand took firm hold. She walked forward, head held high. All the men in the room were staring. Cullen's mouth dropped open.

"Hello good sirs. Forgive my tardiness. King Cullen asked me to attend last night so I could provide answers to those who had them. I'd also like to understand how our councils differ so I can accurately report to my king in Erainn."

"Aye, that I did." Cullen eyed her discreetly and motioned for her to take the empty seat closest to him.

She took the seat right away. Some lords greeted her, and others remained silent. When Cullen spoke. A lord she was unfamiliar raised his hand.

"Sire, are you sure a lady in the council is... acceptable?"

Cullen glared in his direction. "Lady Aoife is part of the Elders Conclave in Erainn. While the concept is foreign here, we should take this opportunity to grow our alliance and learn from our friends."

Aye! Several council members agreed. She hadn't seen that coming. She sat quietly, listening to their concerns, but waited for Cullen to urge her to speak.

Most of their responses felt tempered because of her presence, while others weren't shy with their views on the fae. They wanted to trust, but the curse was fae created. She cleared her throat, and the King turned to her.

"Is there something you would like to add, my lady?" he asked.

"No, I cannot make the men in this room trust me by word alone."

Murmurs filled the chamber at once. All eyes locked on her. "Actions speak for themselves, and I am here to assist in any way that I can," she said firmly.

"Thank you, lady Aoife. I am sure many of my subjects here will take the offer to heart." He smiled and returned to speaking about the curse, then dismissed the council. All besides her. He strolled to the window, keeping his back turned while the men shuffled out.

Aoife remained sitting for several minutes before she stood and started to walk out.

"Wait." Cullen commanded, his tone low and drawn out.

She stopped in her tracks and rotated to face him. His back was facing her when she turned. Waiting for him to yell at her, she took a sharp breath. Whatever price she had to pay for this, it was worth it.

"I thought we spoke about tempering our actions?" he asked.

"No, you did, not I. If you think keeping me locked in this infernal castle and hiding me away from your council will save me, *you're wrong.* If my father knew what you were doing, he'd be irate. How can the people learn to trust me?"

"I told you to give it time." He growled.

"Time is not on our side Cullen." She reminded him.

"Your highness." He corrected her.

"I'm a princess, and not beneath you. How dare you think you can continue to poke and prod me?" She glowered in his direction.

"Dylan, take her to her room."

She fumed at his stubborn distrust, having proven herself time and again in the weeks since arriving in his kingdom. Yet still he shut her out, excluding her from any meaningful participation.

Dylan guided her to back down the hallway, but the creak of footsteps behind her signaled Cullen's approach. She whirled to face him, eyes flashing.

"Why do you insist on treating me like an unwanted outsider?" she demanded.

Cullen sighed. "It is not about you personally, Lady Aoife, but a matter of caution. This council has seen betrayal from within before. I cannot afford blind trust, even in an ally."

"Yet you expect mine in return? While denying me the slightest voice in determining my role here? Was the goal not to become an emissary?"

"You overstep the boundaries more oft than I care for," he said sharply. "You are here at my allowance, and you would do well to remember that."

Aoife drew herself up, chin raised in defiance. "So, you lied to my father then? Am I your prisoner? I am not a subject you can command or dismiss at will! I came because our kingdoms must stand together, not to be made into some ornamental prize on display one minute, then locked away."

Cullen

With that, she spun on her heel, leaving him alone in the corridor. Cullen drug a hand through his golden hair, curse words on his tongue. In truth, her fire and tenacity intrigued him. But he had meant what he said: betrayal had come from those once counted as friends. He could not risk the same again, not with his kingdom balanced on a knife's edge.

Glancing back down the empty hall, he wondered if she was right that he asked too much, while offering too little trust in return. With a weary sigh, he strode off to make amends before her temper flared further.

TWELVE

CULLEN

All Remains the Same

Cullen watched Aoife storm off, her mahogany blonde hair swaying furiously around her. He dragged a hand over his face, cursing himself. Pushing her away was unwise, especially with so much at stake.

Swallowing his pride, he headed toward her chambers to make amends. Her temper was justified, she had proven trustworthy, and he still kept her at arm's length.

As he raised a hand to knock, hurried footsteps approached. "Your Majesty!" a guard called. "Urgent news."

Cullen turned, dread pooling in his stomach at the guard's grim expression. "What is it?"

"Wildfire, sire. Several acres of the northern forest. It rages out of control."

Cullen swore under his breath. Their kingdom was prone to such fires this time of year when rains were scarce. But for one to be sweeping unchecked through the woodlands with the curse in tow and resources already stretched thin...

"Ready my horse," he commanded. "I will assess the situation."

The guard rushed off as Cullen cast a frustrated glance at Aoife's door. Her apology would have to wait as duty called, and as king, he could not ignore his people's urgent need. Regardless of how Aoife felt about him at that moment. He knew she understood the duty he had to his people, as she had given up much to be here herself in the name of her own.

With a silent promise to make things right between them soon, Cullen hurried off to join the fight against the ravenous flames now threatening his lands. The knot in his chest warned of a long and arduous battle ahead.

Aoife
Fall Ascends

Her back was to the door when she heard the guard call out to him. He had come to say something more... but what? Shortly after, a small note was hand delivered. It read: *I'm sorry*. She held the note softly in her hands and tucked it into a small purse for safekeeping.

A letter came later that the curse and wildfires were consuming all his time. Riordan and Dylan were her only company for a solid month. Word had come that the twins were still on the mend and that had brightened up the gloomy days she had become accustomed to.

She wondered... Why was it taking so long and why had her healing been slow? Aoife wasn't sure how much more she could help with the curse either without seeing the infected areas for herself, but Cullen declined to let her see them in person. She had asked him one evening in passing, and he vehemently refused.

He also made quick appearances at lunch or dinner, never staying long. He'd talk about the fires, the lords who were slowly beginning to trust but would leave abruptly and not talk with her again for days. She wasn't sure how they were supposed to learn to work together with the little time they spent together.

Riordan told her later that the curse was spreading like the raging wildfires in the southern part of the land, and the people were in an uproar. Being king obviously meant he had to respond to all the lords in Nairn. Day after day couriers or the lords themselves turned up, begging for the crown's help. Cullen also feared for her safety, so she remained in the castle where he claimed she was safest. She felt more and more like a prisoner with each passing day, and the walls became suffocating.

She even offered to write to her father and ask for aid, but he said no to that too. Aoife sighed and walked away. Riordan told her that some humans held a deep distrust for her people because of the history of the first Realm Wars. She understood their reservations, but the wars had happened four hundred years ago. Humans were proving to be like fae in more ways than one.

Riordan chuckled when she said that and agreed that humans and fae were more alike than they cared to admit.

"If we could all set aside our differences, we'd be

well on our way to beating this curse together," he said.

She agreed. Next on her agenda was appealing to the lords in Nairn. Unfortunately, several had refused to let her come to their lands, despite her abilities. She sighed and begged Riordan to change their minds. She again asked about sending a letter to her father.

"Let me ask him to send the dragons. The drakes are perfect for stopping the spread and they're smaller than horses. So less intimidating. Tell King Cullen. My father will say yes if I'm the one asking. We could also dispatch a small group of our finest healers. If provisions are needed, we can provide support.

"The lords fear the dragon fire will spread too fast. But I'll speak with him this evening and see what he says."

"Riordan, dragon fire burns hotter than man-made. It will not spread."

"I know," was the only thing he said.

He was silent after, so she hurried back to her room while he followed close behind her. She was so tired of trying to help and getting nowhere.

She didn't speak to him when they entered her chamber. He stayed for a bit as she read from the history books he'd brought her. He had always been kind to her, and she was sorry for taking out frustrations on him. But she wanted the quiet of the room to soothe her warring mind.

Riordan finally got up and bade her goodnight. She whispered it back before he left. She was relieved to be alone and soaked in the tub before turning in for the night.

The weather cooled as fall approached. For two weeks, she only caught a glimpse of Cullen in his seat. A line of subjects trailed out into the courtyard and down out the gates. They'd steal glances here and there. A small smile always formed on his lips whenever she caught his brief attention, and she couldn't help but return it.

She waited for her summons to see the Wolf King, but they informed her that the curse spreading kept him busy.

"Too busy to visit his own ward?" she crinkled up her nose at the Druii.

Riordan pursed his lips. "More people come each day. Unlike the fae, most humans don't have magic."

"I noticed this. You're the only one here that does. The cook. She has something. Can't quite put my finger on it. The way she focuses on every item she creates. It's not like yours, though."

"Iona has a bit of magic, I agree."

"Are we headed there now? The kitchens, that is."

"Yes, let's go."

She skipped ahead of him and rounded the corner. Her excitement got the best of her, and she rammed right into the king. Their bodies met, and he caught her up in his arms as they almost fell.

"Oof! Lady Aoife?" he exclaimed.

"King Cullen," she spluttered as her cheeks went red.

"Are you okay?" he tilted his head down and crooked an eyebrow up at her.

He steadied himself, but kept his arms wrapped around her body. She didn't move. Instead, she turned her focus on his face.

"Where are you going in such a hurry?" he asked before she could speak.

"To see Iona."

"Ah! Makes sense. She's quite the cook."

He took a step back, but his hands still touched her upper arms. His thumbs stroking her bare skin.

"S-she is. Almost on par with Orla. Never tell my godsmother I said that she'd be furious," she giggled nervously.

"You have my word." He cleared his throat and

leaned against the wall. When Riordan tapped his forearm, Cullen swiped his hand away.

"I apologize for not visiting. There is a lot going on." He tilted himself closer to her.

"I promise, as soon as I have finished reviewing the requests from my subjects, we'll have dinner and discuss our next move. More lords are ready to trust. I can't wait to discuss it further with you." He licked his lips and moved closer.

"I'm looking forward to it," her breathy voice squeaked out in response.

"I suppose I need to get back to my duties." he inched closer. "We'll talk later." He promised.

She swore the blue in his eyes intensified with each heavy breath she took. Her attention was completely on him. She reached out and touched his arm. His fingers grazed hers.

"Uh Hum! We'll take our leave then. Your highness," Riordan snapped out.

"Of course. We shan't keep you any longer." Her eyes were now on the druid.

His arms laid across his chest. He reminded her of Orla when she was about to scold her, but she refocused on Cullen.

Cullen bowed low, took her hand in one of his and kissed it. He slapped Riordan on the back before he said goodbye and headed out. She thought he would topple over from the force of it.

Riordan shot a dirty look in Cullen's direction while he straightened out his robes and fixed his stance.

"Sire, before you go. Any fresh news on the children?" he inquired.

The king whipped around and frowned. "Sadly no. I suspect we'll have news soon enough. We need to be patient. They are alive and healing. That is all that matters."

"Of course, my king. We'll speak later during counsel."

Once the Wolf King was out of earshot. Riordan gently grabbed her wrist. "What was that?" he whispered close to her ear.

"What do you mean?"

"Don't be coy with me, girl. You and my king. Never mind. Let's go." He looked past her.

He took off walking fast to the kitchens with her hand in his. She looked back and saw Nat for a split second before they disappeared around a corridor.

Iona greeted them with the biggest smile and a plate of apple tarts and tiny bowls of soup. "I made this one especially for you, my dear. I added barley and oats with the vegetables. No meat, like you asked. Somewhat like pottage stew minus the pig."

"Thank you. I appreciate the extra time spent on my food, Iona. Your cooking is magnificent."

"You do me too much honor. I give my thanks in return."

"Lady Aoife is not wrong. This is your best yet!" Riordan plopped a piece of fresh bread in his mouth.

A new servant helped them out to the garden with trays of food for lunch. Efi sat down and rubbed her hands together, bouncing in her seat. She was ready to eat. The druid chuckled and grinned. Then they said a small devotion. Well, he spoke the words she didn't. But out of respect for his customs, she closed her eyes and waited for him to be done. Then they both dug in and filled up their hungry bellies.

THIRTEEN

AOIFE

Plagued By Nightmares

THE NEXT MORNING ARRIVED, AND SHE DREADED THE day ahead of her. Nightmares plagued her with restless sleep. She woke worried about her unicorns and fox friends in Erainn. Would something bad happen to them? The dreams were so vivid.

Someone tortured the foxes in front of her and another cut off Nightwind's horn. Was this a vison of things to come? Or her own mind? When premonitions struck her—though rare—it was usually a warning she couldn't ignore. How could she attend dinner with the king tonight with thoughts of her friends meeting a gruesome end?

If she declined, would he be upset? Would he really make her go without dinner? *What an odd thing to deny me if I don't show. Maybe he spat out words just to get a rise out of me and that was a month ago, so maybe I'm being silly?*

Aoife also wondered if she could appeal to him to let her visit home for three days, but she doubted he'd say yes with so much going on. She wasn't sure it was worth bringing up at all. Riordan would take her dreams into account, but she feared Cullen would dismiss them.

She would have to think of another way to check on her animal friends in Erainn and quick, but what were her choices?

Riordan's knock at the door brought her to the present. She welcomed him inside and readied herself for the day's events. Though they were the same day in and day out, she grew to appreciate the simplicity of each thing on their agenda.

And the gardens, albeit small, were well kept and restored her energy. Aoife pocketed some food scraps for the raccoons and stuck them in the pear trees. They'd climb the vines to her balcony in the evening sometimes and she enjoyed their chattering.

She asked Riordan what he thought about attending dinner, and he said she should go, but was he saying it to appease his own king? When they left her room to take their tea in the garden, she saw Nathair in the hallway in front of them.

Her eyes rolled up, and she knew he wouldn't let her by in peace. Sure enough, he said something. The curse was unstoppable and time for her was running out. She balled up her fist, but Riordan noticed and took her hand into his.

"This way, lady Aoife. We'll take the back way today." He turned them both around and they walked down the servant's staircase and right through the kitchens.

The cook was barking out orders when she noticed the two of them come down.

"What's this?"

"I am sorry, Iona. Pretend we're not here. We'll be out in second," Riordan apologized.

Aoife looked at her and mouthed *'Nathair'*. Iona must have understood and gave them a curt nod as they made their way out the door.

They sat down and drank their tea. Riordan asked her if she was unwell. "I'm merely tired," Aoife claimed, leaving it at that. They walked back up the way they came after they were done. She couldn't stop thinking about the dreams. Or old King Whelan and what she found within his very veins. *Or that daemon. What did they want from me?* They had hidden their identity. The memories of the forest were hazy and distant.

She reached behind her head to the back of her nape. The bump had shrunk but remained. So many mysteries to uncover. Nathair had been right. Time was running out. If they couldn't build up the ties between the two kingdoms, dark days would come.

I wonder if someone started that fire in the Northern Territory? Cullen had said there were people who couldn't be trusted. Enemies deep in the seat of his council, but who? Is there any way to find out?

Sensing her unease, Riordan asked, "What's the matter?"

"I fear what is coming. What if we can't stop it? And what if my healing didn't take? The children die, King Whelan too?" she cried.

"Aoife, the children are fine. King Whelan remains the same. Worry not. We will figure this out," he reassured, patting and squeezing her hand.

"I hope you're right. Thank you for being so kind to me," she said.

"And I appreciate you enlightening me about your people."

Riordan seemed to be the only person with a sense of reason, but she reminded herself that not all humans had magic like fae did. What made sense to her, and the druid wasn't anything a human without magic would comprehend.

"I wish the king and I conversed like you and I do. Is he always so gruff?" Aoife wondered.

"Unfortunately, yes. I'll be surprised if the man ever secures a wife."

"How old is the Wolf King?" she asked.

"Not much older than you. Twenty-five, to be exact."

"Oh, he seems *much* older."

With that, Riordan laughed heartily. Unsure of what was so funny, she asked him why he was laughing.

"Did I say something humorous?"

"Oh yes! I find it hilarious you thought him older, like a grumpy old man," Riordan chuckled.

Aoife giggled as well. "I suppose yes."

"Trust me, it says a lot about who he is. Old King Whelan's been sick since he was eighteen. Prior to this, he lost his mother, sister, and brother to a human plague. He took over at twenty. The weight of the entire kingdom rests on his shoulders."

"That is awful. And his father has been sick for this long? How is that possible? With what I told you about his sickness?"

"No idea. I hope we can figure out the answers soon."

"Me too. Why does he put so much on himself? What about his council members?"

"Ah, you'd think the council would help, but there are too many secrets among those men," Riordan explained. "Cullen is an honest man like his father. Many times, others have tried to ruin them. He is harsh because he must be, to survive, to prevent the kingdom from crumbling. I believe he acts so because evil would see him weakened and destroyed. And he won't let that happen."

"Couldn't he get rid of the council members who wish him ill? Are they truly as evil as you speak?" Aoife asked.

Riordan sighed. "I wish it was that easy. Whelan's laws still stand, so those men have till the end of the year before it's the boot to their arses. I'll be glad when the day comes. Not soon enough, I might add."

"Human court seems complicated. It all sounds so dreadful."

"It is," Riordan agreed. "The Conclave of Erainn sounds much simpler in comparison."

"Yes, and I find myself missing it more than I expected." Aoife admitted the tug of homesickness gripping her heart.

"Missing home?" he asked.

"Yes, can we retire to my quarters? I think I'd like to read for the rest of the afternoon."

"Certainly." Riordan said, as he guided her back into her room and led her to the chair by the fireplace.

"You wanted some more books to read, yes? I had these brought up while we had tea." He pointed to a large stack of books on the table.

"Thank you." She hopped over to them and stroked the covers with her fingers. She was excited to learn more about the human world through these tomes.

"I'll see you tomorrow. Good luck tonight." Riordan added, as he reached the door. He was almost out before she caught on to his words.

"Good luck with what?" Aoife asked, bewildered.

"Dinner with the king."

"Do I have to go? I'd rather remain here this evening."

He shook his head. "No, but I recommend you go. Both of you need a proper discussion after the latest events in the kingdom."

She sighed, "Fine, I will see you tomorrow then?"

"Aye." Then he left her to her own devises.

She looked through the books he had sent up and hoped for one on his Druidry. History, tales, and poetry. No books on human magic. *How did he learn if there weren't any books? By mouth? In person only? Or maybe you had to pass a test in order to see these records?*

How strange. The fae were different. There were records for everything. Even the elders had written the forbidden magics in large black thick tomes.

How did they combat evil without such records for others to read? She wondered? Aoife tried to focus on the books he sent, but her anxiety kept building. She wasn't sure about dinner and wanted to refuse. The confines of the castle had taken their final toll. She had to forgive the humans for not realizing she needed to be with wild things to fill her cup.

Still, if she refused when Dylan showed up, would Cullen come storming in again? For someone who claimed to have such control, he sure had a hothead, too. She hadn't minded his rough touch, and she wanted more of it—as twisted as the thought was.

Maybe she'd purposely wear her nightgown and refuse to change, or maybe... The wheels in her mind kept churning with more bad ideas. She smiled and kept reading.

FOURTEEN

CULLEN

Where is *that* girl?!

News from Bearsden had arrived in the late afternoon. The children were up and doing well. Eating properly, playing outside, and everything. The ranger he sent had followed his directions. They met outside the castle walls, far from prying eyes and ears.

"And what of the forest? Any changes?" Cullen asked his subordinate.

"We did as Riordan suggested, but it's spread further east. This curse, this disease, whatever it is, is hard to contain. We are working as fast as we can, sir."

"And what of the fae kingdom?"

"Certain regions have been cleared. The border

that shares Loch Mora has not. The damned poison overran half of it."

"Are Torin's people there working on it?"

"Aye, sir, I saw them the other day when I was heading to the Stepping Stones. One of them greeted me and said the situation had not improved on their side like they hoped."

"This is worse than I thought. Take your men deep into the woods surrounding Loch Mora. Search for clues, anything, and bring your findings to Riordan."

"Yes sir. Right to it."

"No rest? Surely you can fill your belly and supplies before you leave?"

"If my king commands. Otherwise, I'll take my leave. No time wasted." He lowered his head to show respect.

"You know yourself better than I. Do what needs to be done."

The ranger beat his fist on the left side of his chest, and Cullen responded in kind. He slipped back into the forest like he hadn't been there at all.

If Torin's people were struggling to contain this, what did it mean for his people? *Starvation and death?* Would Erainn help if food stores became limited?

He didn't want to rely on his ally too much. Riordan was the only druid in his kingdom. The others had disappeared some time ago, and not another soul born in Nairn possessed the Druii.

When the situation with Aoife dies down, I bet I can secure more help from Torin when she goes home. It's the only thing that makes sense. Hopefully, Nat will stand down, but I doubt it. We need to find proof of his betrayal, and fast.

Cullen made his way back up the steps and entered the great hall. Empty save for a few members of the King's counsel discussing the affected lands. He walked past the tables in hopes they'd let him be. He was almost up the staircase leading to the living quarters when he heard his name called.

"King Cullen!"

"Yes Grannd?" Cullen spun around and headed back down the steps.

"Do you have a moment to spare?" he asked.

"I take it this is a pressing matter?"

"Of course, sire, I'd never dream of bringing petty things to you this late in the eve."

"Speak freely Grannd. I'm listening." Cullen motioned for him to come closer.

The Counselman looked around with a suspicious eye.

"Sir," he whispered, "I've caught wind of a plot to overthrow you. I have my spies looking into it as we speak."

"By whom?" Cullen leaned in closer.

"You know, sire. Be ready with your most trusted forces. I've sent word for my bannermen to join me here in three days' time."

"Thank you for informing me. The men at the table with you? On your side?"

"Yes, sire. They are aware and doing the same."

"Thank you Grannd. I appreciate you standing with me."

"Always. You were meant to lead. The great Wolf King."

"Your faith is not misplaced. I always try to do my best and will continue to do so. I'll alert Dylan and Riordan, but be wary... have your men set camp outside the city walls hidden well in the trees to the south. Wait till I give you the word. We don't want to alarm the enemy."

"Yes sir, I'm on it."

"I must take my leave now. Thank you again, my friend."

"Always my king."

The men at the table lifted their mugs to him and shouted,

"Long live the Wolf King!"

Cullen honored them with a bow of his head, but jogged up the stairs to his rooms. He slung the door open and plopped down at his dining table.

"Roy, escort lady Aoife to dinner immediately."

His servant quickly left and returned with a red-faced Dylan behind him.

"Did she give you that much trouble, man?" Cullen asked.

"No, she's gone!"

"What!" Cullen jolted out of his seat.

"I can't find her anywhere," Dylan gritted his teeth.

"Fock, that woman. Find Riordan now! Meet me in the courtyard and tell no one. Roy, did you hear? Mums the word?" Cullen harefooted out of the room and back down the stairs.

He walked past the tables and ran into Nat with his three most loyal companions. He wanted to shift into his wolf form and tear that man up. Had he taken Aoife?

"Hail, sire! Where ya headed?" Nat's attention turned to him.

"I am going for a walk before dinner to clear my thoughts, old Nat. I hope you are well."

He hated being pleasant to the man he suspected of treason. Nat stood up and started over toward him.

"The same to you, my king." His words dripped with lies, and Cullen sensed it.

"Thank you. Now back to your meal and no doubt your bannermen are here to report to you. I shan't keep you longer."

"Aye, sire, but are you sure?" Nat's head flinched back.

"We must be prudent in times like this."

"Whatever do you mean?"

"Have you had too much to drink? The curse is spreading faster than ever. Gather their reports and get back to me."

"Oh! But of course. We should speak with this lady Aoife present, for more guidance to beat it?" Nat sat back down.

"We'll speak later and yes, that can be arranged. The advice she offered to Riordan has paid off in Thorn."

"Truly?"

"Yes Nat, it has." Cullen offered a smile before he turned to walk away.

What a nightmare. Seems he's none the wiser on Aoife missing. Where could she have gone? I hope not far. He found Dylan and Riordan waiting in the courtyard.

"We must find her now," using his enhanced sense of smell, Cullen sniffed around as his eyes flickered between human and wolf.

"Caught her scent?" Dylan asked.

"It's faint. She came this way." Cullen's eyes darted to the steps that lead down the side of the castle.

Riordan and Dylan glanced at each other, nodding their heads. Cullen strode ahead, his footfalls echoed off the stone steps. The two men fell in behind their king without hesitation.

"She's probably in the woods." Riordan said.

Cullen's pace quickened. "I'll find her. Riordan, stay here and gather my men. Nat could strike at any moment. Dylan come with me."

"You got it." Riordan flew back up the stairwell with ease and soon he was nowhere to be seen when he glanced back. Dylan was right behind Cullen as they continued down the stairs.

Cullen inhaled the night air and headed south. He stopped at the old hollow tree and peeled off his gear.

Dylan stood watch. His eyes continuously scanned their surroundings for any hidden threat.

Cullen pulled off his boots next. "I'll find her faster once I turn. Keep the area secure. Clear out anyone you find. If I am not back by morning, get the pack together and search for us."

"Got it."

"Only let those in our circle know what's going on," Cullen said.

"Of course. Straight away."

Shedding his pants, Cullen stuffed the remainder of his garments into the ancient tree. His bare skin prickled up as the chilly night air wrapped around him. With a deep breath, he strode purposefully into the dark tangle of trees, allowing his body to transform as he disappeared into the wild depths of the forest.

When he was far enough away, he got on all fours. His arms trembled as the change began. Bones cracked and reshaped, limbs twisting as they bent into new formations. Back arching, he growled through gritted teeth as fur sprouted rapidly across his skin. Cullen dug his hands into the dirt and when he pulled them out, they were hands no more.

A tail popped out of his backside and he yowled in agony as the sound of man mutated to beast. Then he poised his body against the earth, not as Cullen, but as an enormous white wolf. His massive paws sunk into the soft earth. With a shake, he shed the last trace of his human form. From deep in his chest came a rumbling, low, drawn-out howl that filled the air.

He sniffed the soil, moss-covered stones, and trunks of the trees, searching for her. A passing breeze brought the scent he sought. Lifting his muzzle, he caught her trail. Cullen sprinted down a hillside that led into a ravine and followed the trail further south.

FIFTEEN

AOIFE

Hunted by Wolves

AOIFE CLUTCHED THE STOLEN TUNIC TO HER CHEST, inhaling the scent of lavender soap before trudging on. Trousers hung baggy from her hips, but offered more protection than her dresses ever could. The chilly air permeated her flesh as she fixed a long wool cloak around her. *These clothes will have to do for now.*

She had studied maps of Nairn in secret for weeks, tracing her finger along each contour line until the ridges and valleys blurred together. The forest loomed ahead, dense with towering trees that blocked out the fading sun. Southeast was the best path to take to avoid the villages. It'd take her longer to get home, but she'd risk it. Anything to get her friends before her dreams became reality.

She picked her way through thick underbrush, twigs snapping beneath her boots. She came to a steep hill and slid down it into a narrow gorge, and continued south. The light of day trickled slowly away and the path in front of her widened. Night would soon be here, so Efi investigated the trees for a place to sleep. The soft rustling of nocturnal creatures awakening echoed around her while she searched.

A raven flew down and perched itself on a dead alder trunk. Its black eye followed her and it clicked its beak. She used her mind to connect. *Do you know the way to Loch Mora?* She asked. The raven cawed and hopped closer.

Be not afraid I am fair folk. No harm will befall thee. The bird caulked its head to the side and cawed again. Her hand brushed its face, and it rubbed against the back of her palm gently before ascending back into the sky. Its message to her was loud & clear. *Danger.*

Efi slowed her steps and perked up her ears. *Danger,* she repeated as her senses became more alert. There were large predators in the forest that she wasn't sure were friend or foe, but humans could be a threat too, depending on how they felt about the fae. Which one she'd meet she didn't know. Suddenly she heard the low howl of wolves and took off running.

Her feet gripped the small boulders in the ravine as she continued to run further away from the howls, but they grew closer with each stride she took. When they stopped, she heard nothing but the muffled sounds of steps behind her. She looked side to side, then behind her. *Nothing.*

She glanced up, spotting one of them up on the rocky sides of the gorge pacing her, but something was wrong. A thick dark liquid covered its snout and dripped from its mouth and its gray fur had patches missing.

The cursed poison had gotten hold of this pack. *How are they still alive?* She was both amazed and utterly terrified. Their behavior would be hard to predict. So, she did the only thing she could and kept her legs moving and didn't slow down.

Her keen hearing picked up the pads of their feet as they stalked her further into the forest. It got louder and louder with each second, so she whipped around, grabbed some large rocks, and stuffed them in her pocket. She stood up tall and puffed out her chest.

Maybe she could scare them away if she appeared larger than they were. Three of them approached. One in the center, its yellowed eyes on her. She took a deep breath in and stretched herself out more when she released it and growled as deep as her voice could.

She kept her eyes on the middle one as it crept closer. The wolf snarled and snapped at her. She squirmed a little and slowly tiptoed back. The wolf followed her every move. The others stepped in line with the leader.

She eyed the rocky edges of the pass. Were they stable enough for her to climb? Would the wolves try to follow her? Too many unknowns. There could be an end to the gorge soon if she kept running, but not even the speed of the fae would save her now.

The wolf that appeared to be the alpha came closer, so she yelled out and took a stone from her pocket and threw it. Hitting the thing square between the eyes. She threw another and continued to bellow out, trying hard to scare them away.

It shook off her attack and growled out. They were too far gone to back down. She made one last effort and screamed so loud the wolves stopped their ascent, but it was only for a second—a slight backward glance from the leader and the rest gathered closer to him, gaining distance as they approached.

Then a loud, booming howl echoed around the rocky walls that surrounded them all. A giant white wolf jumped into the middle of the pack and thrashed several of them around in its mouth. It tossed them aside like they weighed nothing.

It clamped its jaws on the back end of the alpha and threw it aside. She stood an inch from its face when it turned around. Its blue eyes met hers and she swore there was a familiarity to them.

"You seem to be helping me. Let's fight them off together?"

The pack lined up behind the great wolf. They snarled and snapped. It turned to face them and growled deeply. The sound sent shivers up her spine. They backed off for a moment, but continued to observe her. She had a feeling that the toxin in their veins would only make them persist.

Two wolves lunged and snipped at her new protector. She took more rocks into her hands and hit each wolf that edged closer to them. In a flash, the one she assumed was the alpha attacked and dug his mouth into the side of the white wolf. She punched it in the back and the others soon followed and attacked its other side. She lifted her arms up and beat down into the cursed wolf's back.

"Get off!" she screamed.

Her new companion fought off every single advance, and then they turned their attention to the leader. It took the whole torso in its mouth and bit down hard.

Next thing she knew, the wolf pulled her close and crooked its head back to show she should climb on.

She crawled onto its back and they ran off down the path in front of them.

She hoped the blighted beasts would give up, but she could hear them running to catch up to them. The curse had turned those poor things unnervingly savage and dark. They looked like wolves, but somehow they were not. Whatever had a hold of that pack had destroyed their very being. Animals in nature had a purpose, and they had lost it.

She clung to her savior as it flew through the night with monstrous speed. Never before had she seen a wolf so huge and powerful. Its coat was like a blanket that wrapped around her with warmth and protection. She thanked the gods, whoever they may have been, for providing her this miraculous rescue.

The chase seemed to last an eternity. The cursed assailants kept coming, never letting up pursuit. Efi yelled out in desperation, "*When will they stop*?" she cried out.

The wolf stopped a moment, and she slid off. It faced their enemy once more. "Are you sure?" she asked.

The giant wolf paused, then stepped forward and blocked her view. With a roar that shook the earth around them, it charged headfirst at their adversaries. Claws and teeth ripped through them, splattering viscous blood everywhere. Two of her pursuers were down and only one remained, whimpering in agony.

Efi gasped in horror as she watched the ceaseless battle unfold before her. Closing her eyes tight, she muttered to herself: "Will this never end? I can't take much more of this." Clenching her fists together until her nails dug deep into her skin, thoughts of what Cullen said rushed in. *I need to make sure I aim and hit our attackers. I must have more control over my magic.*

She focused her light into a ball between her hands. She aimed right for the ones who were still attacking and flung it in their direction. The light hit and dispersed, burning the bodies of their enemies. She formed another and chucked it at the last one standing and more shrieks let out.

Some of them retreated, but two stood their ground. Her friend, who she realized was male, came to her side. "Fight together?" She asked.

The great white wolf answered with a low growl and head bowed. She mustered up her light once more, her fingers shaking. This was a lot of work for her, but she couldn't give in. Efi hurled the last sphere at her attackers.

They fell to the earth and stayed down. Her new friend urged her to get up on his back and she climbed right on. They wasted no time in getting away.

The night sky turned ominous, clouds rolling in to blot out the bright moonlight. Eerie howls echoed all around as the pack converged. Still, the white wolf pressed on tirelessly through the gloom—relentless in his bid to escape the enemy trailing behind them. Until they both spotted an opening to a cave.

Slipping inside the rocky opening, she leapt down from his heaving back. The wolf's flanks shuddered with each labored breath, dark blood flowing freely from gashes torn by tooth and claw. He whined, the fight leaving his body. He needed her healing hands and soon, but first, they needed fire.

She looked around for a bunch of twigs and small branches to start it. She built the fire far enough from the cave opening that they wouldn't get smoked out, but also big enough to keep out anything that wished them harm.

Aoife let the glow of her hands illuminate the cave. No other surprises or creatures awaited them. Calling on the faery lights of old three small orbs floated above them and provided warmth: They'd be safe till morning. She asked her hero to come to her and inspected his body. So much tainted blood mixed with his.

"I need to heal you, but let me rest a few moments." She spoke, breathless after the exertion.

He recoiled and growled. "You will suffer the

same fate as your wolf brothers if you don't let me help you." She said, putting her hands around his snout and placing her forehead against his. He tried to stop her at first, but soon he rested his head on hers.

Efi knew she needed to get her light into his body right away. She forced it through her own forehead and into him. He yelped a bit and struggled against her, but she latched on tight.

"Please, hold still the best you can. I don't want the poison to take hold," she whispered, pleading in his ear.

He grunted a sound of approval, and she scanned him for more open wounds. She wished Nightwind was here to assist. The healing would not be a simple task.

"Is there fresh water nearby?" She walked past the fire and studied the dark forest around them. She knew it was a risk to leave the safety of the cave and the fire, but she needed something more to assist her magic. He limped up and blocked her.

"You need to rest. I have never had to heal like this before. Water would help, but it's not necessary. It may take me longer without it."

Her new friend whined and pushed her back into the cave.

"You win. I will stay close by. I need to fuel the

fire. I'll grab those dead branches over there. They are close by."

He snorted and laid back down. She got more firewood and made it burn hotter and stronger. They made their way into the middle of the cave. The orbs following them. She worked on his wounds in small intervals; taking small breaks in-between to save her strength.

Sweat dripped from her brow as she focused all of her healing power to save him. He stopped her by getting up.

"Why did you do that?" He nudged her and cocked his head. A low rumble of content came up from his chest.

"I am fine. Don't worry about me. Lay back down."

He struggled to walk, then toppled over on his side, but he forced himself up on his front legs.

"Like I said, I need to keep going!"

He resisted a moment, but he laid back down and closed his eyes. She checked on him. His breathing was steady, but something wasn't right. She saw a flick of his paws and a jolt from his legs. His whole body began spasming as he thrashed back and forth.

There was nothing she could do but sit there in horror. His snout shrunk, and his white fur fell out around him. The wolf's body shifted more, and she sat frozen in place, both terrified and mesmerized by what was happening in front of her. Yelps of pain filled the cave.

Soon she saw a man lying on the ground and she gasped loudly. "King Cullen, *is that you?*"

He groaned and rolled onto his back. He was completely naked. She bent over, covering her eyes, and took off the cloak she was wearing, draping it over him. She'd never seen a naked man quite like him before. *And never this close,* as she wasn't allowed to frolic about on sabbats with her fellow fae. Aoife took a deep breath to compose herself and continued healing.

She worked on his left arm first. He'd glance up at her and muttered words she couldn't quite make out. Every time she touched him, she felt sparks of electricity pass between them.

When she got to his chest, she unhurriedly slid her fingers across and down his sculpted stomach. He was handsome. Every single inch of him. Her body tingled all over as she leaned in closer to him. His gaze remained fixated on her, and she stole a few glances while her magic mended his flesh.

When she finished his upper body, she blew out a nervous breath. The bottom half was next. Blood soaked through the cloak on his right side.

She crawled over his body, but he clutched her wrists and pulled her down on top of him.

They made eye contact again, and the only thing she could say to him was. *'It was you the whole time'*. He nodded in response before his hands continued to touch her in ways she wanted more.

Her body trembled as he slid his hands up and caressed her sides and leg. His touch was soft and intoxicating, and she wanted nothing more than to drink it all up. His fingers touched her face and slowly traveled down her neck to the top of her breasts, his palms rested on them and a warmth spread from there and down to her core. She shifted her body down and he moved his hips up towards her, but he grunted and she looked down.

"Your leg. We. Um. I... I need to heal this."

"I suppose you're right, stupid leg. I like where you're at right now. Can't you stay?"

She lifted her lower half off him and crouched down beside him. Every inch of her quivered. She gently lifted the cloak up to his groin and folded it over. Efi cupped her hands over the oozing slashes. Cullen winced when the glow of her hands leaked out around and illuminated them.

When she finished, there was a small spot where the teeth marks had been in his skin. Only dried blood remained around them. He sat up and placed his hand behind her head and scooted forward.

He pulled her back onto his lap, and His lips brushed against hers.

"Your highness!" She squeaked, staring deep into his eyes. Her breathing was erratic. He tugged her closer, and she swore up and down her body had a mind of its own. Her lips pressed back into his. Her mouth opening enough to feel his tongue touch hers.

His fingers combed through her hair with one hand and the other held onto the top of the pants she was wearing. Cullen slid his hand down and massaged her bare skin.

His hips ground against her inner thighs. Heat pooled between her legs.

"W-we shouldn't," she panted. "Mmm." was his only response.

He shook his head yes like he agreed, but his hands slid up under her shirt, but he paused. "Sorry, the wolf in me," he said with his head down.

"It's okay." She touched his face, holding it in her hands, and planted a kiss on his check. She rolled off to his side, lying there huddled resting on his chest.

"I'm sorry I ran. It was stupid of me," Aoife admitted.

"I'm sorry for keeping you cooped up. I should have mentioned I'd take you to the woods earlier. But I wanted to surprise you at dinner." He put her hand into his, weaving his fingers through hers and holding on tight.

"I need to admit that wasn't the reason I took off. I sometimes have prophetic dreams and had terrible images fill mine the last several nights. My concern for my animal friends in Erainn outweighed any reason to stay." She squeezed his hand.

"Oh. Not what I expected. I have to take back what I said earlier. Seeing you jump into action to help me when those rabid beasts attacked. You held no hesitation and dove right in to fight. Then you risked everything to heal me. You intrigued me before, but I approached you with caution. I wish half my men had the courage you do, princess." He nudged her with his shoulder.

"You give me too much credit. Some of it belongs to you."

"What do you mean?" he asked.

"You called me brash, that I rush in without thinking, and you weren't wrong. I tempered my attacks so I wouldn't hurt you. You're not human, not fully anyway. What are you?" She chattered away.

"I'm Faoladh. What some call a werewolf."

"That's why you're called the Wolf King." She said with a slight grin.

"Something like that. Most think werewolves are a myth. If they only knew the truth," he sighed.

"Where do we go from here?" She asked.

"Aoife." He whispered.

"Yes Cullen?"

"You're free to leave. I can't keep you here against your will. I'm sorry I even forced it."

"What about Nairn? Ewan and Elsie? Surely you need me to stay?

"Who?"

"The children."

"Sorry, I forgot their names between all the reports and everything going on. Hard to keep things straight," Cullen said.

"No, I'll stay. I need to figure out why your father and the wolves aren't dead from the poison. It might aid in the healing of both our lands," she replied.

"All I can say to that is, *thank you.*" His tone sincere.

"You're not as gruff as I thought you were."

"Don't be fooled. I am tired from fighting off those cursed wolves."

"So, what do we do now?"

"We have a few hours till morning. I say we sleep now and return to the castle on foot. When the sun rises."

"How? You have no clothes."

"I know the cloak has blood in some areas, but what if you give me your breeks and we just keep the cloak around you as best we can since that tunic is down past your knees without the sash tying it up? I'll give them back once we reach the hollowed-out tree near the side castle entrance."

"Why there?"

"I have my own things waiting inside. Though I suspect my men will look for me first. Not sure we'll make it that far. We'll see them before that."

"Are you sure?" She asked.

"Positive."

Efi took the pants off and handed them to Cullen. He pulled them on. They were a little tight and made his bod stick out. She caught herself staring hard before she looked up to see him grinning.

"Are your legs cold?" He asked.

"A little." She confessed.

"Come here. We can lie on top of the cloak," he offered, laying down and beckoning her to do the same. He wrapped his arms around her and pulled her close to him, their noses touching. His body temperature relaxed her.

She nestled against him, soaking in his warmth. "Are you always this warm?" she asked.

"Yes, it's the wolf in me," he murmured into her hair.

"Are you sure we should rest?"

"Yes. I hope you're okay to sleep like this?"

"If it means being close to you then yes."

Howls echoed around the cave walls. "I don't think they've given up. They're trying to wait us out." Aoife worried.

Cullen stroked her arm reassuringly. "We're safe until morning. The fire burns hot." He paused. "I'll be savoring that kiss until the next time. Maybe we can..." He muttered, his voice trailing off as his hand caressed her side. Unable to resist, Aoife pressed her lips to his in a passionate kiss before exhaustion overtook them.

"Seems the adrenaline from fighting and healing has left us. I feel sleep trying to take me," he whispered.

His eyes closed, and soon he was asleep. She stoked the fire before she did the same. There was movement out in the trees and a feeling of unease washed over her and she scurried back inside, watching for anything that dared to edge near the flames. Before she ventured deeper within the cavern, she made sure the fire burned hotter and brighter. She laid down next to Cullen and pushed her body into his, and felt safe. She closed her eyes and soon she drifted off into the nothingness that starts every dreamscape.

SIXTEEN

CULLEN

A Snake Always Bites

THE SUN CAME POURING INTO THE CAVE. AOIFE WAS still fast asleep on the cloak. He stood up and looked outside. He sniffed the air. The cursed wolves were gone. They could head back to the castle safely.

He checked on her for a moment. Cullen wasn't sure what had overcome him last night, but he knew he wanted her more than he did before; he craved her body against his. Still, it was too soon for such things. People would suggest he had fallen for the enemy, but he couldn't deny what he felt from the beginning.

He wanted to give her his wolf, which meant giving all of himself to her and no one else. He'd denied the pull when they had first met, but no more.

Doubt crept into the edges of his mind: Would she really stay? *She said she would*. He hoped she wouldn't change her mind. A small, petite yawn grabbed his attention. He bent down and reached his hand out to her. She took it and he pulled her up.

He spoke first, "Morning."

"That it is. We're both alive," she said.

"We are. Shall we head out? I bet Iona has bread baked and ready when we arrive." Cullen shook the dirt off the cloak and wrapped it around her shoulders.

"By all the Fae, I hope so! I'm starving!" Aoife exclaimed.

"If we go back through the gorge, we walk right by some blackberry bushes. Grab a handful as we walk?"

"Sounds wonderful. I love berries."

They approached the gorge. Blood stains were on the rocks and sand. Cullen sniffed the air, catching the scent of Dylan and the pack.

"Here, let's go a little faster," He urged.

Aoife stepped up her pace to match his, and they continued on their path back to Falkirth. Birds chirped in the trees. Squirrels skittered about and a mother raccoon returned to a small entrance in a bunch of large stones, with her babies trailing behind her.

He watched her squeal with joy at the scene in front of them. He loved it. The smile on her face, the way the light reflected off her skin. He couldn't take his eyes off her.

She smiled slyly and stretched her arms out wide. Her back arched and her chest stuck out. Every move entranced him and she seemed aware, only teasing him more with her every move.

The sun got further up in the sky when he heard loud boisterous voices surround them.

Dylan yelled out, "There he is! King Cullen!"

His men rushed to their sides. Dylan handed him a large sack. Four others approached. Bram, Alastair, Tavish, and Finn. They all patted his back and yapped about how long it took them to find his bloody half naked ass.

"Well, something must be wrong with your noses, ya whelps!" He laughed.

"Aye, we ain't old like you," Tavish jabbed his elbow into his gut.

"We have bad news," Alastair spoke.

"Report then? Dylan, men? What's going on?"

"Nat attacked the castle earlier, right before daybreak," Dylan informed them.

"What? Fock one thing after another!" Cullen sped up, getting his clothes and armor back on.

"Men, we head into battle!"

"I lied and told Irving you left last night to take lady Aoife out to a section of the forest that needed more attention than human hands could provide." Dylan said.

"Thank you. Let's hurry back then." Cullen said.

Aoife took the breeches back and put them on, right in front of his men.

"Turn your eyes, men!" bellowed Bram.

She straightened the legs and tied them up as best she could.

"Fussing over a woman getting dressed! We have more pressing matters at hand, you know! Humans are so peculiar with bodies and nakedness. The fae are different in that regard."

"Well, princess?" he looked at her.

"Yes?" she asked.

"Let's go!" Cullen shouted.

"Yes, out of the frying pan and into a fiery snake pit," Aoife breathed out.

"She's got that right." Dylan said.

They ran back to the castle as fast as they could. It surprised him that Aoife kept his stride.

"When we get to the outside of the castle. Aoife needs to be taken to Grannd's encampment." Cullen commanded.

"Most of his men have joined the fight, but I bet

the old man stayed behind. Waiting for you, sire." Dylan said.

"I won't sit in camp while you all fight!" she protested.

"Aoife, we don't have armor to protect you." Cullen rasped.

"I don't care! I said I'd help you." She insisted.

"I swore an oath to your father to protect you. I can't let you join us."

She huffed and threw herself ahead of everyone. He smiled as she outran them all, even him. *I'm loving this woman's fire.*

He sprinted up behind her when she came to a halt. Grannd was barking orders to his men when they approached.

"Ah, here's our king!" All the soldiers beat their chests and called out.

"We are ready when you are, sir!" Declared Grannd.

Cullen joined him at the war table. "Tell me what Nat's done and what you have planned, Grannd."

"Nat attacked the bridge. He's made his way through the streets. He means to kill you and your father to take the throne. I'd rather slit my throat before I let that happen!" Grannd fumed. His face reddened with anger.

"My men are fighting off a small brigade at this

end. Keeping them from going up the steps." He pointed to the map on the table.

"Good. We'll take some of your men and head up there now. Can you keep Lady Aoife with you while we fight?"

"Ah, the fae woman who can heal the land. Why is she... never mind, I won't ask... It'd be my honor, sire. Brogan spoke highly of you, lady Aoife. It is a pleasure to meet you."

"He did? Pleasure is all mine." She said.

"Aye, that he did. His twins are doing well. Thank you for taking care of my people."

"Glady, I'd do it again in a heartbeat."

Cullen reached for her hand and gently pulled her close. "I'll return. Please stay here," He pleaded.

"I will."

Cullen squeezed her hand. Then directed the groups of men to follow him. He headed out with his men and Grannd's. Their swords drawn and ready.

He turned back and witnessed Aoife watching him as he left. She looked upset that she couldn't join in. Did fae women fight alongside their men? He'd have to ask her after he secured the castle.

SEVENTEEN

AOIFE

Faery Godsmother! Is That You?

"You'll wear the ground down the way you're pacing," Grannd spoke.

"You seem to be loyal to Cullen. I need your help. Do you have any armor that could fit me?" she asked him.

"Strange thing to ask me. Women in Nairn don't fight unless they have to, and they rarely do. Do your women in Erainn take up the sword often?"

"Everyone in the unaligned kingdom does. The courts of faery don't play by honorable rules. They'll do whatever it takes to subdue." She couldn't believe she was spouting off the very things her father taught her. She had always questioned his words, but with the cursed forests and animals... there was no doubt in her mind what they were capable of.

"I see. This is troubling. I dare say Nat is a small contender compared to what's out there."

"I think you may be right, sir." She said.

"Once Nat is out of the picture, we can sway most of the lords to our side. We need each other if we are all to survive this curse on our lands."

"Agreed."

Grannd had a decent head on his shoulders. She was glad of his company, though deep down she wished she had her armor and short sword to join the fight against that horrible man.

"I wish Orla and Cillian were here right now. They would know what to do." She whispered. Just then, the winds shifted, and a faint whistle traveled through the arms of the trees. Aoife couldn't put her finger on it, but something had changed right after her wish.

She asked if she could walk around camp a moment to wear out her nerves. Grannd said yes, of course, and reminded her to stay close by.

A creeping sensation trickled up her arms and through her back. A familiar flash of periwinkle blue darted into a tent. With some haste, she made her way to the entrance and lifted the flap to enter.

Sitting on a cot was none other than her

godsmother. Holding a small box in both hands. A warm smile on her face.

"Orla!" gasped Efi.

"Hello my dear. You called for me, so I am here." Orla crooned.

"But how?" Aoife asked.

"A fairy godsmother cannot reveal all her secrets. I brought Cillian with too."

Next thing she knew, Cillian appeared in the tent. He looked at Efi, his eyes and mouth wide open.

"Close your mouth, boy. You'll let the bugs in if you keep staring like that," Orla said in sharp fleeting tones.

"Efi? What happened to you? Are you hurt? What in Nine Hels are you wearing? Where am I?"

He fussed over her after giving her a deep hug.

"Cil, I am fine. The situation is worse than we thought. Worse than you can imagine. The curse has been here in Nairn for years and now a traitor has attacked Falkirth."

"Orla, get us all home now. Father be damned!"

"No." Efi's voice was calm and firm.

Cillian frowned. His head shaking side to side. He didn't want to accept her answer. "No, you're coming home now!" he demanded.

"I need to stay," Efi pushed back.

"No, do you even know what father agreed to with that man?" he protested.

"I do. Fate led me here. I must see this to the end."

"You can't mean this! You truly wish to stay? Despite everything?" Cil asked.

"Yes." She confirmed her answer once more for him.

"Aoife, I don't like this. You're still the princess of Erainn." Cillian reminded her.

"This is my choice to make. Didn't you say to face my fears and grow up? This is my chance, brother." She urged him to see it was the right thing to do.

"Not like this!" he exclaimed.

Orla walked up between the two of them and handed her the small box.

"Everything you need is inside." She held her hands tight around Efi's before pulling her into a deep hug.

"Thank you. Your magic never ceases to amaze me, godsmother." Aoife beamed.

"Cillian. You and I will take our leave now." Orla placed her arm through Cillian's.

"But Orla." He stammered.

"Cillian, your love for your sister is very strong. Lend her that love for what comes next. She will need every ounce of it."

Cil groaned, "I still don't like this. I could stay and fight. I hope you know what you're doing, Efi."

"The people here barely trust me. Adding you to the equation isn't a good idea. I can't make such a promise to you, but I will try." She offered.

"I guess trying is better than nothing at this point." He reached out to hug her with his free arm.

"In the beginning, I didn't want this either. I hated the idea of being stuck with humans, but now it feels like I belong here, so here I stay," Aoife said.

Cillian's lips pursed. Worry written all over his face. Orla chided him for resisting what his sister wanted. Efi smiled while she listened to them argue. Torin was her father, but Cil was her twin.

It pained her to tell him he couldn't stay and help her. She saw no other way.

She reiterated her promise to stay safe one more time. They both knew it was a lie, but he finally accepted, and Orla's streams of sparkling white magic swirled off her fingertips and danced around him until his body vanished.

Orla sighed. "I know what you plan to do. You want to fight with him like you did in the woods."

"How do you know that?" Aoife's face twisted with confusion.

"Your father may have forbidden me from coming with, but I've watched over you all the same. I waited for you to call out, but you didn't until now." Orla smiled warmly before pulling out a tiny black box.

"I don't know what to say other than thank you. I'll remember to call out to you directly next time. What is this trinket you have?" Aoife asked.

"Remember this dear. A blood oath is serious. I would never dishonor your mother that way. Yes, the call must be spoken aloud. You must always say you need me right now. It's the only way it will work. Here, take this." She said, handing Aoife the tiny box.

"Thank you again."

"Go show these people we are their friends. I fear what I've glimpsed from watching you... it is merely the beginning of something bigger. It writhes around in the deepest dark. It lies in wait for its taint to consume, so it can devour Nairn and Erainn whole until we are no more."

"This is overwhelming." Efi's head hung low.

"I understand. You've had so much happen in such a short time. But I have doubt you'll figure everything out." Orla reassured her as she took Aoife into her arms and hugged her tight.

"I best be off. Go bind that snake."

As soon as the last word trailed off her lips, Orla dissipated into thin air. She studied the small box in her hands. Orla's voice filled her mind. *Everything you need is inside.* Efi pried the lid off and picked up a single dragon scale. Right underneath the scale was a small carved sword, only an inch long, with tiny boots and pants. Each item trembled within her grasp. One by one, she sat them out in front of her. Each quaked on the ground and grew in size.

Her eyes lit up when she realized it was her armor and short sword. She wasted no time getting her gear on. She stuck her sword in the sheath and headed outside. Ready to join Cullen by his side.

Aoife whipped by Grannd in a flash. He cried out when she flew by. An enormous grin on her face, and she winked at him before she disappeared up the castle stairs.

EIGHTEEN

AOIFE

Catching A Snake

She snuck past a small skirmish with Cullen's men. They made fighting look easy. Nathair's men never stood a chance as they lay moaning in agony on the ground. She made her way through the kitchens undisturbed, staying hidden from the skirmish just outside.

She'd go through the servants' entrance to the living quarters. Cullen would head straight for King Whelan. The kitchens were quiet. Almost too still to her liking. She crouched down and slinked up against the long prep tables.

Iona wouldn't have left her area for just anyone. Sure enough, she had stayed behind. Her labored breathing giving her position away. Efi crawled over and asked if she was okay.

"Lady Aoife? Is that you? How'd you get in here?" she whispered.

"I snuck by. Can you tell me what happened?" Aoife asked.

"They attacked the gates, and then old Nat stormed the castle with his men. He was heading up the stairs to your rooms and found them empty. Riordan sealed himself and several guards in old kind Whelan's room."

"So, they're safe for the time being? Did you see Cullen come through?"

"Last I saw, he went up to dispatch old Nat. I hope he guts him good. If Nat got word, he might have retreated to the great hall. You was smart coming through the kitchens." Iona added.

"Thank you, Iona. Stay here. I'll be right back," Aoife reassured her.

"What do you mean? You need to stay here!" Iona pleaded.

"I can't. Don't worry about me." She smiled.

"Miss, I am prone to worrying. Nothing anyone can do about that. I can't stop you either. You look like you can take care of yourself. Good luck." She took Efi's hand into hers and held tight.

"Thank you," Aoife said.

She whispered *goodbye* to Iona and snuck up to the doors leading out to the great hall. She creaked one open. Cullen's men had Nat and his lackeys pinned in the center of the room.

"Give up old man! You've lost!" Cullen barked.

Nat remained quiet. His sickening grin made her stomach lurch. She studied the scene before her. Cullen's men blocked the front and side entrances along with the stairs. Nathair's men stood in a circle with their swords ready.

And that coward stood in the center of all of them. Nat's lips curled up, and he pulled up his father by the arm. Cullen's men stomped closer.

"I'll slash his throat if you take one more step!" Nat pressed a dagger into the neck of old King Whelan.

Cullen put his arm out and held Dylan back. She had never seen Dylan so angry, but the Wolf King remained unnaturally calm. Nat had his father trapped. There was no way to surprise the snake on his end, but no one had seen her yet.

If she sprinted at the right moment and ran up the bench to the table nearest to them. She could vault over the circle of men and right into Nat's ugly face.

This has to work. She bent down and pressed her feet and fingertips into the floor. One leg behind to push off with full force. She inhaled deep before she released all her strength into her sprint. Her eyes on the table in front of her as she sped right to it.

NINETEEN

CULLEN

It's a bird... It's a... It's Aoife!

When I get my hands on old Nat, I'll strangle him to death with my bare hands. Cullen's nostrils flared. His shoulders stiffened and his jaw clenched. The worst had happened. Nat had grabbed his father and took him hostage. By some luck they made it in time, so Da was still alive. His opponent's sickly yellow eyes flickered with gratification while his lips donned a devil's grin.

Cullen knew Nat wouldn't spare his da. Cullen had no idea how he'd save him without being stabbed to death himself. There was no way he'd let Nathair take the last of his family. *Not today.*

"Give up old man! You've lost!" Cullen growled.

you'd ever be, a far better man, too. Who cares if the Ostraige Tales are true? We've gone three hundred years in peace!" Dylan shot out.

"Aye!" several men shouted.

"Will you still think so highly when the old mad king rips out yer throats!" Nat jabbed back.

Then out of nowhere. A flash of muted bronze and gold flew right over the heads of Cullen and his men. Straight over the circle of traitors who harbored the snake, Nat.

"Sire! Look up!" his men shouted in unison.

"It, it can't be." His eyes grew large and his mouth dropped open.

Nat didn't know what hit him. All Cullen saw was her dark blonde hair flowing around her as she kicked her feet into Nat's chest. His back hit the ground with a large thud. Her lean body crouched over him. A short sword slid out from Aoife's side and she pressed it up against his neck in a flash.

"Tell your men to surrender and drop their weapons!" Aoife scowled.

"Look, the little faery princess. Yes, I know who you are and you're too late," Nat mocked.

"I'll slit his throat right here, right now." She warned, digging her blade into his neck.

Dylan yanked at Cullen's arm. "Sire, what do we do now?" he gulped.

"I have no clue, but if Nat moves even an inch... I think she'll do it."

Nat, still on the ground, began laughing hysterically. "You're too late, the lot of you."

His men looked at him for their orders, but he didn't stop. Aoife shook him with her one free hand and then hopped up, sword still close as ever. She dug one foot into his chest.

He spat at her and glared, "Mark my words. Kill the fae princess men, and I'll double your earnings." Nat said.

"Aoife, stay there. We are coming!" Cullen yelled.

One of Nat's men swung his sword at her, but she flashed out her light from her free hand and hit him in the face, blinding him. His skin turned red and blistered up in seconds. He screamed in agony, his hands pulling at his face as flesh peeled off, revealing muscle in its place.

"Make it stop! Make it stop!" he squealed.

The man took off running and slammed right into the wall, crumbling to the ground. Nat's men glanced at each other; their faces pallid. Aoife lunged forward a bit, and they all jerked back.

"I dare you all to try." Aoife said.

She gets sexier by the minute. How's that possible? Focus, you idiot, Cullen thought. Some men immediately laid down their weapons and even seemed glad to be escorted away by his men. He could see Nat stewing in his defeat.

"You fools! How dare you betray me! Over a fae woman! A weakling!" Nat belted out.

He tried to get up, but Aoife wouldn't let him. She slammed him back down every time he moved.

"Just wait. You think you've won, but you haven't. This is only the beginning." He scurried across the floor.

"You're the one pinned to the ground by a woman, Nat." Cullen gibed.

He noticed her looking down at his father. His limp body sprawled out against the cold stone. He feared the worst. What had been in the vial? Da's body began shaking with such violence everyone moved back.

"All of you will see." Nat

His father's limbs bent and his face grew long. *Fock! He's changing! Nat has figured out how to force shifting. Is he a druid? How did he hide this from us? I need everyone out of here now.*

"Aoife, back down. Men, shields up! Be ready! Back out of the hall," he bellowed.

Only a small group of Nat's men stayed with their leader. None seemed eager to engage Aoife, who refused to move. The rest had run off as soon as they saw his father changing.

Black hair sprouted out from his body, his clothes ripping with each change to his form. His human flesh shedding off. He was seconds away from being in full wolf form.

"Damn you Nat," Cullen snapped.

"Cullen..." Dylan's voice faded.

"Be ready to hold him back at all costs," Cullen ordered. Tavish and Bram bolted over to where he stood. He was relieved to have more backup. "Take the left side, Tavish. Bram on the right. Dylan, follow my lead," he said.

Cullen's father was now in full wolf form. Snarling and snapping his jaws at the men who stayed. They swiped their swords out at him, but missed every time. With one swipe of his paw, he had knocked four men down.

He studied his father to guess his next move. A black substance dripped from his nose and covered his gums. Aoife had been right. Whatever had cursed the wolves had cursed his da too.

Cullen refocused on the scene before him. They closed in on them. Nat was losing allies. More of his men fell and others retreated. Cullen was close, but right as he pushed a soldier out of his way, his da faced off with Aoife.

"Stay still, don't move!" He stressed.

She nodded her head. Nat scrambled up off the floor and stood next to her, his eyes on Whelan.

Cullen had seconds to act and threw himself in front of her. Tavis and Bram flanked his father's sides. Dylan got behind and waited for orders.

Nat slowly backed away, but then his eyes had a devious look about them. He whipped out a knife with a green stained blade and slashed up Aoife's side.

He took up his sword and tried to stop the next advance. Everything moved in slow motion. Nat muttered some incantation and swiped at her side again. This time, he didn't miss. The blade slipped in between the scales and she cried out.

"I dipped that blade in poison. There is no way to save you now!" he cackled.

Nat pushed her down and ran. Cullen watched, frozen in position as his da followed. Whelan snapped at Nat, who retaliated and picked up a sword from the ground.

Nat screamed out, "Damn you werewolves and fae alike! Humans are all that matter. I won't see this kingdom in the hands of our enemies. Soon, the Maleficary will return and take what is rightfully ours."

Whelan pounced and then tore into his enemy. He bit down on Nat's sword arm, disarming him. Nat shrieked out in pain. Not a single man lifted a finger to help him. He was getting what he deserved.

Finally able to move freely, Cullen hurried to Aoife's side. She stumbled into his arms and he held her tight. She pressed her hand against the wound and brought it up. Covered in blood.

"I think I am okay. It doesn't seem like much." Her were words soft as she spoke.

"Riordan will fix you right up. He's coming down the stairs." His voice shook.

His father turned around and faced them. Blood soaked his fur as Nat's body lay still. The light made the dark red wetness glisten. He didn't attack, but nudged Aoife with his snout.

He was aware. *Thank the Gods.* A faint smile crossed her lips as she reached up to touch his head. Her hand was already glowing bright gold.

"Aoife, no, you don't have the strength." He tried to stop her, but it was too late. Her connection to his father was unbreakable. His da's entire body lit up.

"I'll be fine." She murmured before her hand dropped by her side. Her body going limp in his arms.

Cullen checked her breathing. It was stable for the time being. He fussed over her some more before he sensed his father communicating. *She's healed me. You need to save her now. Take her to the border and call out*

"I'll slash his throat if you take one more step." Nat's sickly smile grew wider than it was before.

Cullen's men jolted forward, and he pressed his arm against them to hold them back. "Stay back men!" He implored, "Stay back!"

They stopped in their tracks. Old Nat smirked before he dug his fingers into Whelan's arm.

"Why are you doing this?" Whelan croaked.

"Because animals shouldn't rule." Nat bit out.

Cullen took in a breath. *Don't react.* Mumbled voices carried throughout the hall.

"Silly old man. Folktales and myths." Cullen responded.

"You can't hide anymore, Wolf King. Neither can your father. Men stand ready!" Nat crowed.

He's trying to goad me into changing. Stupid little man believes he'll force my hand. Cullen remained stoic and silent. He wouldn't give Nat the satisfaction, but he was a tricky sort. *What does he have planned?*

Nat whipped out a small vial from his pocket and forced it down his da's throat. Cullen sprung forward but was met with the tips of swords. One nicked his right cheek as he dodged back, wiping the blood from his face with his hand.

"Here soon everyone will see that you've lied and I tell the truth!" Nat sneered.

"And so what if he lied? He's a far better king than

for the unicorns. Trust me, son, they'll come. Go, Riordan and I, we will make sure everything is okay here.

"Men, I must go! All of you witnessed her heroics today! She fought for humans when she's fae. I need to help her! He took one more look at his father as he held Aoife close. Da was walking back up the stairs. Riordan at his side.

"Take care of him my friend," Cullen belted out.

"Of course, my king," Riordan said.

"We'll head to Grannd's encampment. There'll be horses ready to mount." Cullen shifted Aoife in his arms.

Aoife moaned. Her body was feverish and sweat beaded along her forehead. He headed out of the great hall and down the side of the castle, back to camp. His feet barely touched the ground. He glimpsed Grannd as he whipped by. He got to the horses and Dylan followed closed behind.

"Stay here. Make sure everyone knows we've stopped Nathair and his men." Cullen said, before turning back to Aoife, checking her feverish state once more.

"Go! I got this," Dylan urged.

Grannd came sprinting towards them, his face a mask of worry. "I heard everything. Take the black one. His name is Obsidian. He's feisty, but fast and focused. He'll arrive there in no time. Bless the poor lass, I commend her for fighting. Gods speed my king."

Cullen stepped forward and took the reins with one hand before swinging himself onto the horse's back. Dylan assisted Aoife onto the horse, and Cullen wrapped an arm around her waist to keep her steady as he clicked his tongue and squeezed his calves into the horse, urging it to move faster. The stallion's hooves pounded against the ground as they galloped down the Beaten Lane, illuminated by the fading orange light of the setting sun.

TWENTY

AOIFE

Darkness Inside and Out

THE BLADE SLID BETWEEN HER ARMOR AND STUCK INTO her side. After that, everything turned into a haze. She reached for old king Whelan. Golden light. Searing pain. Blood? Her blood. Cullen scooped her up and carried her in his arms. *Where are we going?* The ceiling of the great hall morphed into the late afternoon sky.

Soon, all she sensed was his warm body touching her. First, she was hot and his body heat made hers boil. Next, she was freezing. Her teeth chattered and her body shivered all over.

Cullen whispered to hold on. She tried to tell him

she was all right more than once, but her words slurred.

"We're almost there. Hold on a little longer... for me." He told her.

The stars in the sky above spun round and round. Then the darkness took her.

The sound of Cullen's voice filled her ears. Her vision blurred. The dizziness she had earlier remained. A pain shot through her side vibrating out to her chest, shoulder, and legs.

"It hurts," she sobbed.

"We're close. I have you." He tried to comfort her, but his efforts seemed in vain.

She could feel the gallop of the horse they were on.

"I am glad we are not far away. One fast horse is all we need." He reassured her.

"Me too. I can't see a-and the p-pain," she croaked.

She tried to hold her head up, but unconsciousness threatened to take her again. She resisted and tilted her head back into Cullen's chest. Her body ebbed and flowed between hot and cold once more. No relief in sight. She didn't know how much more she could take.

All she wanted was to do was to see her home again. Months had passed since she had left Erainn.

Her soul ached to view even the smallest part, if only for a few minutes.

Home. She curled her fingers around Cullen's cloak. His scent filled her nostrils. His gaze briefly met hers. The edges of his face were fuzzy, but his eyes she could see clear as day. *I don't want to leave. I am drawn to him, to Nairn. I must stay. Please let me live.* She pleaded to the Gods in silence.

The poison continued to ravage her body as intense stabs of pain shot through her arms, neck, and face. Her side went numb as she gasped for air. Touching the wound, she raised her blood-coated fingers. It contained streaks of black and bright green throughout.

"What manner of poison is this?" she choked out.

Cullen answered, "I am not sure. My father told me to get you to the border and call for the unicorns to heal you."

"What if they don't come?" She squeaked.

"Then I'll ride all the way to Erainn's palace." He vowed.

Her head lolled back, limbs and torso going slack in Cullen's arms

"Aoife!" he cried out.

She wanted to answer, but she was too weak. Her lips barely moved. The night got darker. The road disappeared and dark swirls of blue swallowed her whole as she slipped unconscious.

TWENTY-ONE

CULLEN

Save the Girl

CULLEN TIGHTENED HIS HOLD ON AOIFE. SHE WAS OUT cold. Her breaths were short and shallow, but her heart was still beating steadily. He wanted to stop and check on her, but they were so close to their destination.

The road curved sharply, then straightened back out. The great stones came into view and he shouted for help.

"Unicorns of Erainn. If you can hear me, please save your princess!"

They came to a halt right in front of the boulders that made up the boundary. When he dismounted, he took his time in getting down so he didn't hurt her as they got off. He yelled out again, calling for them. Cullen held her in his arms before he placed her on the ground.

He inspected her wound right away. The moment he saw it, he knew she had lied. The laceration was worse than she claimed. Blood was oozing out and pooling around the scales of her armor. He undid the leather straps on the sides and removed the front piece. He ripped into her blouse and tore a sizeable chunk of the fabric off to put on her wound, pressing down to stanch the bleeding.

Her whole body remained still as her skin grew colder to the touch. He calmed his nerves and concentrated. *Still here.* He combed his fingers through her hair and touched her face with one hand, hoping it would help her wake. Her skin drained of color and her lips were pale. Visions of his mother and siblings dying flashed before his eyes, and his hands shook. *I barely know her, but I am pulled in her direction. Please Gods give her mercy. What if what I feel is more? Don't take her, not yet. You have already taken so much.*

"Aoife, hold on. Just a little while longer."

He scanned the other side of the border. Nothing stirred between the brush. Cullen kept pressure on her wound and talked to her. Told her where they were there and what he was doing. He kept shouting for the unicorns, begging for their help, but no one came.

He had to decide and fast. He didn't want to waste precious time if they didn't show. Cullen whistled and directed Obsidian to his side.

"I guess we'll have to ride on, boy. Can you do that for me? Gods, she has to make it. Please, if you're out there, help us! Heal her! She's your princess!" exasperated Cullen.

His shoulders slumped and his head hung low. His arms reached down to pick her up, but his eyes caught sight of two bright lights approaching. Cullen's mouth dropped. He had never set eyes on a unicorn before, let alone two. Their coats shined like pearls in the moonlight. They were tall and lean. Taller than any horse he'd ever seen.

Their manes sparkled like starlight, and their violet eyes pierced into his soul when he caught their gaze. One was male and the other female. The male approached; nostrils flared. He reared up, coming down hard to the earth and stomped his hoofs.

The female nudged Aoife with her forehead before she examined her head to toe. Cullen watched as his curiosity peaked. No one in Nairn had laid eyes on a single unicorn. This was a first.

A deep voice filled his mind. *Are you him? The one they call the Wolf King. I am Nightwind. The princess is a dear friend. We came as fast as we could. Dessa will heal her. Be not alarmed when she does. Remain calm.*

"What do you mean?" Cullen asked.

He didn't understand the unicorn's request until Dessa put her horn four inches into the cut on Aoife's side and a groan escaped her blue tinged lips. He sprung forward, but Nightwind blocked him and knocked Cullen over before he could reach them.

Do not interrupt! Stay still. Whatever she does, you can't react to it. Has to be done this way. You are Faoladh. I thought humans ruled this land?

"You can sense what I am? How long will it take to heal her?"

Tell me what happened first. It's hard to know until we begin. The scale armor Aoife wears is impervious to damage. How did she get hurt?

"A lord of my court wanted the throne for himself and attacked my castle. Near the end of the battle, Aoife had him, but he's always been a tricky sort. Apparently, he was a Maleficary, but hid it well. He said some sort of incantation and the blade slid right into her side. The blade was dipped in poison too." Cullen said.

Magic and poison. Both are tricky. I may need to join Dessa. Promise me you will not move while we heal her. I know how it looks and I won't lie. It is painful, but the end result is what matters.

"I promise. It shocked me and I reacted. Sorry, I will control myself."

No apologies are necessary. I can see you want to protect her as much as we do. I would have questioned your honor had you not lifted a finger.

Nightwind joined Dessa. Cullen held his breath as the unicorn put the tip of his horn into Aoife's chest. She yelped in pain and her back arched up when his horn lit up. There were no tales or records of how unicorns healed, just that they did. What he thought they would do versus reality left him speechless.

Their horns lit up. He expected white, but it was a bright silvery light. Threads of this silver light coiled around her body. They started out from her chest and side wound and flowed outward, wrapping down round her arms and legs.

Aoife's skin pulsed with a faint glow all over. Each wave of healing that traveled through her body made all her muscles spasm. Her hands and feet twitched uncontrollably.

He had to look away. Her writhing body tugged at his memories of his siblings and mother dying again. He forced a deep breath and glanced up. He hated the feelings of helplessness then, and he hated them now. What was so great about his wolf's blood if he couldn't help the ones he cared about?

You got her this far, and you were willing to go farther. Your actions matter here. The unicorn clan does not forget.

Dessa pulled out her horn. The wound sealed up. The flesh mended and closed up. Nightwind stepped back. A small droplet of blood clung to Aoife's chest.

"Is she? Is she all right?" he asked them both.

He crept closer and grabbed one of her hands. The stab wound was nothing but a scar with tiny woven flecks of silver throughout. He stroked it with his finger and cupped his hand on her side.

He paused what he was doing and focused on her, to sense her breathing. The soft lull of her chest rising and falling with each shallow breath brought him hope. When her breathing got stronger, he grazed a finger against her lips.

She inhaled and then released. Her eyes creaked open, and she blinked with a smile on her lips.

"Aoife. Thank the Gods."

He reached for hands and pulled her into a tight embrace.

"Cullen," she rubbed her eyes, looking around. "Nightwind and Dessa too!" She exclaimed.

"All here, they healed you." Cullen said.

"You've saved my life twice now. I owe you." She murmured in his ear.

"No, I owe you."

She tried to get up and stand, but lost her footing. He caught her, of course, and she relaxed in his arms.

"I don't think you are quite ready for that," he chuckled.

She looked up at him. "I guess not. What's next?"

"We're by the border. You could go home. You've gone through so much. I can't ask you to come back with me, but I want you to stay. No, pay no mind, you should go home."

"Aye, I agree. Let's head back to Falkirth once I can stand," she chirped.

"Are you sure?" He asked.

"Positive." She nodded.

TWENTY-TWO

AOIFE

Two Kingdoms Two Homes

NIGHTWIND AND DESSA RESTED THEIR HEADS ON HER shoulders. She rubbed her cheeks to theirs.

I will miss you both so much. I cannot thank you enough.

Dessa's airy voice permeated her mind. *I thank you. You saved me from that daemon. Oh, princess, I hope we see you again soon.*

I promise to make a trip to the border as soon as I can. They nickered in her ears before they turned back to Erainn and headed out. It was hard to be so close to home, but she had work to do.

Nat was gone, but the dark fae were still out there.

That daemon she called the shadow being was also around. She had sensed it deep in her bones, trying to ignore it. What came next would be a mystery.

She could finally stand, but Cullen helped her up on a black steed he called Obsidian. They took their time riding back to the Falkirth. He talked of things rapidly changing and he was hesitant to return.

"They saw my father change. Now everyone in Nairn will know what we really are." He sighed.

"Don't worry. Your family has done a lot for the people here and they are the type to not forget. I read that much in the library. You have people loyal to you as well, like Grannd. Let's not forget those other men too." She reassured him.

"You're right. Maybe we'll be fine." He added.

"I think we will be. We have so much to discuss, too. I didn't even sense that Nat was a druid, but I don't know what a Maleficary is, do you? He hid it so well. The only thing bothering me is, he claimed he was for the humans only. Does that mean he wanted all others dead? Your da told me he knew Nat had something to do with his illness, too."

"Interesting. I don't have a clue. Unless he thought he could keep control of others without issue?" Cullen suggested.

"The daemon I crossed paths with. Its touch

instantly infected the trees. What if Nat summoned it? Then forced it to do his bidding-infecting your father. Maybe he thought he had the upper hand sending back to its realm, but my father said that daemons are part of Faery. If summoned, they'll keep returning, even if the caster thinks they've sent them back because the gateway is on the other side of the mountains."

"Did he tell you anything else?" He asked.

"No, he seems to keep information from Cillian and me. I'll be honest, I hate the secrets. I'm sick of them," she remarked.

"Me too. Let's take a vow. Honesty from here on out." He declared.

"Aye!" She smiled and agreed.

"Well, we are almost back to the castle," he released a sigh of relief.

"I can't wait to set foot in the kitchens to see Iona." Aoife said.

"Me too. I bet you she's cooking, even with everything that's happened," he said.

"It's her magic." Aoife pictured Iona kneading the bread. Whispering that tune she always did.

Cullen hugged her waist tightly and clicked his teeth, sending Obsidian into a trot. She looked up at the sky and gazed at colors changing to sunrise. The rest of the ride was quiet. Small chatter here and there.

When they got to Falkirth. Grannd and Dylan were waiting with all their men. They didn't take the side entrance but lined up and walked through the main gate and into the street.

Whispers of the great Wolf King taking down the snake reached their ears. Citizens in the streets bowed low and bellowed out.

"Long live the Wolf King! Long live King Cullen and his father Good King Whelan!"

She hadn't seen the city up close. Only from the castle's balconies. Aoife heard them talking about her and how she had helped saved their kingdom.

Loud cheers and clapping followed them all the way to the castle gates. When they opened, Riordan rushed up to them and helped her down.

"Let's get you upstairs to rest," Cullen said.

"That sounds lovely." Sleep tugging at her eyelids. Cullen helped her up the stairs, and Riordan followed behind them. They got her to her room. They said they'd check in later and left her to relax.

The events of the last couple of days danced in her head. Some of it felt so unreal. She washed the blood and grime off her skin. Her hands dipped into the washbasin and squeezed the rag out and draped it over the edge. The exhaustion became stronger by the second. She dried off and placed a thick night gown on despite the sunlight in her room. A small fire crackled in her ears and she dozed off sitting in the chair, watching the flames flick up around the burning logs.

TWENTY-THREE

AOIFE

"I Will Always Find You."

A brisk breeze whipped through her hair. The fire had died down to embers. The day was gone. She got up from the chair and headed straight for the pile of firewood next to the hearth. Her neck was sore from sleeping on it wrong. She kneaded the tightened muscles as she dragged her feet across the floor.

Her eyes adjusted to the dark surrounding her while she plucked two small logs from the basket in front of her. She noticed the balcony doors were unlatched and the breeze that woke her earlier turned into a wind blowing the doors wide open. A familiar cold slipped up and wrapped around her arms and back. She dropped the wood and hurried out of her room. Dylan was standing watch when she flew out the door.

"Princess, are you all right?" he asked.

"No, would you check my room, please? I think somebody is in there with me." She shuddered from the cold still seeping into her bones.

His facial expression changed as he called for more guards to come to her room.

She stood in the hall biting her nails when Cullen peeked out from behind his door before stepping out. "What's going on?" he asked before joining her at her side.

"I think, no. I woke and got scared. Dylan is checking my room," she said.

"Will you be all right?" he asked her.

"I think so? I don't know." She told him honestly.

Dylan came out and looked at both of them. "We searched every inch of your room, Lady Aoife. We found nothing. I am not sure what scared you. Beside the balcony doors, everything else is untouched. I'll have my men scour the outside just in case, okay?"

"Sorry Dylan, I thought maybe it was..." her words trailed off.

"After what you've been through, I don't blame ya for reacting the way you did. I will always check for you. Even if I find nothing," he replied.

"Good, good. Glad it's been sorted." Cullen yawned.

""I think both of you should return to your rooms if it's all the same." Dylan ordered, speaking as a friend and not a guard.

Cullen let out a small laugh.

"Sire, back to your room right now, then. I don't want another Nat incident." He directed scooting Cullen to his door.

"I thought I was the king here," Cullen chuckled.

"Still, I would like to make sure you stay king while protecting lady Aoife too. I'll have Finn come stay with you," Dylan spoke.

"Ya heard the lad. I'll see you in the morning." Cullen walked back to his room and stood in the doorway. He teetered side to side.

"I will have the rest of the soldiers conduct a thorough search of the grounds, too. No stone untouched." Dylan had never been more serious.

"You never disappoint. This is why you're the head of the guard." Cullen added before he closed the door.

Dylan saluted him, then ushered Aoife back into her room. She studied him while he got the fire burning bright again.

"Thank you," she squeaked.

"You're welcome. Back to bed?" he suggested.

"Yes."

"I can tend to the fire. I'll be right outside for the time being." He offered.

"I appreciate that. Thank you." She smiled up at him.

"When my men report back to me. I'll come back in and stay in the chair." He added.

She let out a sigh of relief and thanked him again as he helped her back into bed and returned to his post. She pulled the blankets up around her chin and settled in.

The light of the flames pranced off of the walls attempting to loll her back to sleep. She resisted the urge to close her eyes completely. Her mind focused on the feeling she had earlier. She wanted to understand why she had it, if there was nothing... no one in her room.

The cold she had felt wasn't the nip of the cool night air. Nor the bite of winter reaching out, letting her know snow would fall soon. Nor a random breeze that trickled across her skin. No, it was neither of those things.

What she perceived was something she had pushed far back into the recesses of her mind, but she laid there with it, creeping in and taking hold.

If she thought about it, would she be calling the thing to her? Or would it come all the same? She stared at the ceiling while the shadows played tricks on her.

She pinched her eyes shut and refused to open them again, but something lightly grazed the front of her cheek and stopped near her ear. What only could be a tongue wet and warm glided up the side of her neck. She bolted up searching the room but there was nothing.

Just Dylan fast asleep in the chair. Windows and doors unopened. Her heart pounded in her chest she could feel the thumping in her ears.

"I told you in the forest I'd always be able to find you," a voice whispered.

"Show yourself," she commanded.

On the edge of the bed, a bare chest and torso of a man appeared out of thin air. Bright shining eyes peeked out from long dark hair as more of the shadow being became clear. Sleek, long fingers gripped the blankets, tugging them off her.

"Dyl-" she sputtered.

A large hand reached out and choked her, keeping her quiet.

"Shhh. I'm only here for a minute. You wouldn't want to waste the opportunity to hear what I have to say by waking your guard would you?" the daemon smirked as he slowly released his hold on her.

She tilted her chin up and kept still.

"How did you get in here? What do you want?" she seethed.

"Straight to it. You're marked by me. What do you think I seek?" He purred into her ear as he touched her leg.

She recoiled from his touch, and he dug his fingers into her knee.

"No," she managed to eke out.

"I will have what's marked. What's mine," he growled.

"Never, I am not yours to keep!"

"We'll see about that." He hissed as he flicked out his tongue at her.

"No, get out. I'm not afraid of you!" She snapped.

The shadow being tilted his head to one side and grinned. A tendril of smoke curled up around his body as he dissipated. The last thing she saw was his sharp teeth glistening before he disappeared entirely.

Dylan bolted up out of the chair bewildered, his sword drawn out, but it was too late the daemon was already gone.

"Aoife, I had the strangest dream. What are you doing awake?" he asked.

"Nightmares."

"My dream it felt so real. I swore I had this twisted creature sitting on my chest, holding my arms down, keeping me from moving. You were there in bed and this man with long hair he had you by the throat. Gods, it was horrible," he cringed.

"That sounds terrible. I'm sorry," she replied.

"Aye, I'll be fine. What about yours?" He sat back down, alert, and scanned the room.

"I am not sure. Don't worry about me. I am sure we will be better in the morning."

Dylan agreed and folded his arms and closed his eyes.

She watched him doze off and picked at the blankets bundled up around her before she fell back to sleep.

TWENTY-FOUR

AOIFE

Must Have Been a Dream

THREE WEEKS HAD PASSED SINCE THE BATTLE OF Falkirth took place, and all seemed quiet in Nairn. Aoife was still healing. She stayed in her room most of the time to preserve what little energy she could muster.

She helped Riordan search the records for anything on the Maleficary, but they found nothing so far. Like the very thought of dark druids died with Nat. They'd still look through the archives. After all, she couldn't do much else.

Afternoon tea quickly became her favorite part of the day. Riordan helped her to the garden, and Cullen carried her back to her room. She sat by the fire with another book and he joined her. The memory of the night with the daemon had faded, and she convinced herself the whole thing was merely a bad dream.

She told no one since she couldn't be sure it was reality. Cullen had hot apple cider brought in, and they each took sips from thick clay mugs. Dylan and Finn were standing guard outside. The castle was quiet, ushering in winter.

"Those snowflakes falling outside are quite large! I haven't seen but tiny flurries!" she exclaimed.

"I hear Erainn doesn't get as much snow as Nairn does. Is that true?"

"Yes, that's true. Erainn has mild winters we get snow, but it never sticks and always melts the next day. I think it's all the magic we've brought to the land."

"Ah, then soon you will have a scene to behold. Lots of snow is in your future. We'll have to show you how Nairn enjoys the winter with our snowballs." A mischievous smile spread across his lips.

"Snowballs? How much snow? What is it like?" she asked.

"Cold, wet, but fun to play in. I think winter is beautiful though. We need to have some proper clothing made and taller boots too. Are you okay to wear fur?" he asked next.

"Will I need to? Is velvet not enough for here?"

"Oh no, you'll need layers of wool and fur to keep you warm. Especially up here on the mountain."

"The fae don't mind wearing the skins of animals, but we try not to unless the animal has given us express permission before they pass on. Our custom is the same with eating meat too. Though I refuse to." She spoke.

"I will make sure we find a seamstress who understands your needs."

They both went back to reading. Cullen would peek up from his book and study her as she read. She kept envisioning a sharp toothed grin next to her face and a wretched hand on her knee.

Why the dream persisted into her waking hours eluded her. She told herself for the one hundredth time. *It was only a dream.* A terrible one as it still haunted her waking hours.

I am sure that's all it was. A horrible nightmare, nothing more.

It was only a dream.

The End.

ABOUT THE AUTHOR

Adalynd (otherwise known as Alexis to some) is a wife, mother, author, and designer. Adalynd writes Romantic Fantasy with varying degrees of spice and a bit of darkness sandwiched in-between.
Hoarder of craft supplies, coffee cups, yarn, bandanas, and books. ***A*** loves tacos, tea, and toast (with cinnamon & sugar). When she's not momming, she's writing, creating, gardening, DIYing, and for sure playing her favorite video game Fallout. She's pretty introverted but can be coaxed out of her cave with the promise of good conversation and tasty food.
She also enjoys spending time with her family and has been married to the love of her life for fifteen+ years.
A currently resides in the majestic state of Arizona (her homeland) where she keeps her eye out for spicy land lobsters, has a growing petting zoo that includes chickens, ducks, cats, dogs, salamander, a red bearded dragon, and one cute white rabbit too.
She hopes you'll take a walk in the forest of her

imagination and join her as she wanders through her worlds and stories.

AUTHOR'S NOTE

Dearest Reader,

You've made it to the end of the story. I look forward to sharing further installments as there is much more to tell! If you enjoyed this book, please consider leaving Given to the Wolf King a review.

Every review helps the author get their books to more readers. All because of YOU, yes you. Each review matters! I'll take them all from one to five stars. Feedback is invaluable and helps me grow as writer.

I also encourage you to subscribe to my bi-monthly newsletter so I can get to know you. If you sign up, you'll get writing updates, sneak peeks, character art, special newsletter giveaways, and much more.

Grayves Garden Newsletter
Find me wandering around the web here:
Adalynd Grayves

MORE BY ADALYND GRAYVES

Want to read other works by Adalynd? Check out them out below:

Bounty

Calypso's Song

Dark Souls

www.ingramcontent.com/pod-product-compliance
Lightning Source LLC
Chambersburg PA
CBHW020241030826
48979CB00030B/2372/J
* 9 7 9 8 9 8 8 9 5 4 0 1 9 *